The Curious Case of
SEAMAN GARBER

Also by B. K. Mayo

Tamara's Child

The Water Tower Club

The Curious Case of
SEAMAN GARBER

B. K. Mayo

FIR VALLEY PRESS

Library of Congress Control Number: 2021923312

ISBN 978-0-9815884-1-4

Cover design by Betty Martinez

Printed in the United States of America

Published by Fir Valley Press
Roseburg, Oregon

To contact the publisher, send an email to:
info.firvalleypress@gmail.com

In memory of my dad, Oscar O. Mayo,
Staff Sergeant, U.S. Army, whose ashes reside,
along with my mother's, at the San Joaquin Valley
National Cemetery in central California

1

THE TWO BOYS HUFFED from a delicious blend of effort and anticipation as they dragged their home-made raft down the embankment to the water's edge, its skid path resembling the imprint of some heavy-bellied beast slinking down to the pond to quench its thirst.

The raft consisted of a deck of wooden pallets that the boys, using nylon twine, had lashed together atop a couple of inflated truck inner tubes. Though cumbersome to maneuver on land, once in the water it rested on the surface as neatly as a lily pad.

"Think it will hold us?" Seth said. He was hunched over, hands on his knees, eyeing the make-shift craft with uncertainty. At eleven, he was youn-ger and smaller than his companion, and more cautious by nature.

"For sure," Collin said. He stood erect, gripping the push pole he'd fashioned from a fir sapling with his hatchet. "Go ahead. Get on." Collin was twelve. Having descended from a long line of timber fallers, he possessed the self-assurance typical of men who worked in the woods.

Seth took his time complying. He didn't mind playing Robin to Collin's Batman; he just wasn't going to follow him blindly. There was a red line of danger he chose not to cross. Although he had to admit that at times he allowed Collin's spirit of adventure to overwhelm his better judgment.

This, however, did not appear to be one of those occasions. Their newly launched craft seemed seaworthy enough. And after all, these weren't the roiling waters of the Pacific. This was a manmade reservoir used in the past for storing logs. How perilous an undertaking could it be?

Setting aside his reservations, then, he stepped aboard the buoyed platform. To his relief it remained afloat, dipping only slightly in the water. He shuffled around on the wobbly deck and faced his friend. Collin was smiling, but then Collin was always smiling. Seth tossed up his hands in a gesture of triumph.

"Here we go then!" Collin cried. Prodding the raft with his pole, he shunted it away from shore and bounded aboard.

The abrupt addition of Collin's weight caused the linked pallets under Seth's feet to teeter, and he lost his balance. Just when he thought he would tumble headfirst into the pond, the raft settled into a gentle bob on the water.

"I told you it would hold us," Collin crowed, his grin as wide as the Grand Canyon.

Seth was thrilled. He wheeled around and pointed like an ancient seafarer toward the middle of the pond. "Onward, mate!"

Collin needed no prompting. He dug his push pole into the pond's floor and propelled them into deeper water.

The boys had worked on the raft nearly every day since school had let out in mid-June. Now it was almost July. The inspiration for the project had come one day when, using machetes to clear blackberry vines from around the old watchman's shack set on the high ground above the pond, they found a heap of wooden pallets buried in the brush.

"Hey, I've got an idea," Collin said as he dragged out one of the pallets. "All we need is some twine and a couple of inner tubes." That was how most of the boys' adventures began—with Collin getting an idea.

Sunlight shimmered off the water like sparkling diamonds now as Collin, plying his pole like an experienced ferryman, sent the craft in an undulant crawl farther away from land. Seth steadied himself on the ever-shifting deck by spreading his feet and crouching, his exuberance tempered by a sober reappraisal of the danger involved in this enterprise.

The pond, long since abandoned by its owners, Southern Oregon Lumber Company, was the boys' favorite hangout. Their families had lived for many years on acreage bordering the log compound, Seth's to the west of it and Collin's to the east. In the summer months, when the sun rose early and bedded down late, the boys spent as much time at the pond as their daily chores allowed.

They entertained themselves by chasing quail through the tall grass beyond the fringes of the pond, or *being* chased by wild turkeys. They tramped along the shoreline, tossing into the water the bulkiest objects they could find—boulders, chunks of deadfall, rusted machinery parts—to see who could make the biggest splash. They skipped flat stones across the pond's surface in a contest to get the most bounces. Barefooted with pant legs rolled up, they waded into the shallows and scooped up tadpoles with long-handled nets made of kitchen strainers wired to broomsticks. And when they tired, they sat on the bank squishing their toes into the mud, watching ducklings dabble by or buzzards circle overhead or deer dart out of the brush at the sound of a rifle shot in the distance.

They had done all these fun things and more. But before today, they'd never ventured onto the pond.

"How deep do you think it is?" Seth asked as he peered into the murky water. But it was like trying to see through a wall; he would have needed X-ray vision. They had gone beyond the quilt of lily pads and cattail spires that rimmed the shoreline. Swarms of mayflies and water striders scudded across the pond like a moving smokescreen. He could see the tops of weeds below the surface and here and there a branch from a dead tree limb poking up through a patch of moss, but he couldn't see the bottom.

"Probably no more than a few feet here," Collin replied, attentive to his task. "Deeper out in the middle, no doubt." Off to the right, a paddling of ducks, until now gliding peacefully through the water, skittered away from the encroaching hulk and its passengers.

As they crept toward mid-pond, Seth scanned the

far shoreline. It was as deserted as the bank they had left behind. It used to be different, Seth's dad had told him. Years ago when the lumber company shuttered the local mill and stopped using the pond for stockpiling logs, they stocked it with rainbow trout and allowed company employees and their families to fish here. It was especially popular with the kids, Seth's dad had said, because they could almost always count on experiencing the electric thrill of hooking a fish and the pride of holding up their catch for the camera.

Then one spring day, a six-year-old girl drowned in the pond. She was the granddaughter of one of the mill's supervisors, whose unemployed and inattentive son had come to the pond with his fishing pole, his young daughter, and a six-pack of beer. A lawsuit followed, and upon its settlement, the old log compound was closed off to everyone.

In the years since, the no trespassing signs and wire fencing kept most people out. But Seth and Collin knew every spot where the fence could easily be crawled under or hiked over. The pond, with its central location between their country homes, its seclusion, and its lure as something forbidden, had become their private playground.

"It's getting deeper," Collin said.

Seth felt a stitch of anxiety. "How deep?"

Collin pulled his pole out of the water and stood it up on the raft. It was wet to the height of his armpits. "About four feet, looks like." Above that, about another six feet, the pole was dry. "No problem, I've got plenty of pole."

But Seth, nearly a head shorter than his friend

and not as strong a swimmer, wasn't concerned about the length of the pole. He was concerned about his own length.

"Should we go out any farther?"

"Why not?"

Seth didn't have a ready answer, at least not one that wouldn't make him sound like a wimp.

It didn't matter; Collin already had the pole back in the water and was leaning against it. But this time, the craft, instead of plowing ahead as before, pivoted in place. The next thing they knew, the raft had spun around to face the direction from which they had come.

"What happened?" Seth asked, confused.

"Don't know," Collin said. He lifted the pole out of the water. "Trade places with me."

The boys edged past each other on the wooden planks. More deliberately now, Collin dug his pole into the pond's bottom and set his weight against it. But again the raft made no headway. It merely swiveled around as if anchored in place.

Collin frowned. "We must be snagged on something." He laid the pole on the deck, dropped to his knees, and peered down between the slats.

Seth squatted beside him. "See anything?"

"Just moss and stuff," Collin said. "No—wait—there's something . . ." He poked his hand down between the slats and groped around. "I was right; something's caught us. Aha!—a tree branch. There—I've got ahold of it."

Making a face that reminded Seth of a snarling raccoon, Collin tugged on the branch and continued tugging until he'd wrenched it free from where it had

6

become jammed between the two layers of slats. Now it protruded up through the deck, near the raft's center.

Collin wiggled the branch back and forth. "It must be attached to a limb that got buried in the mud."

"So what do we do now?"

Collin rolled his shoulders as if he were a wrestler loosening up for a match. "We gotta break it off. But we gotta break it low enough for the limb to let loose of us." He moved to the edge of the raft, lay down on his belly, and hung his upper body over the water. He glanced back at Seth. "Sit on my legs."

"Why? What are you—?"

"It'll keep me from falling in."

Finally understanding, Seth straddled Collin's legs.

"Put all your weight on me," Collin said. He laughed. "What there is of it."

Seth wasn't amused. "I weigh seventy-two—"

With a sudden lurch, Collin plunged his head and his right arm and shoulder under water, leaving Seth struggling to provide the counterweight needed to keep his friend from sliding off the tottering raft. He stayed submerged long enough for Seth to become concerned, then came up gasping for air.

"Can't reach it," he said between pants. He sat on the raft catching his breath, his face shiny wet, his hair spangled with pearls of water.

Seth eyed the errant branch scornfully; a thought came to him. He stood up and tugged on the branch. It showed more of itself and then receded when he let go of it.

"I've got it," he said. "Let's pull it up as far as we can, break it off, and then push what's left back down. That should free us."

"Worth a try," Collin said, rising. He secured his footing and gripped low on the branch.

Seth grasped it higher.

"On three," Collin said and started counting.

On three, the boys tugged. The raft dipped in the water.

"Pull!" Collin urged.

The raft dipped deeper the harder they pulled.

"I'm pulling as hard as—"

With a screech resembling that of a barn owl, the branch came sliding up through the slats. The boys grinned at each other in satisfaction.

Then the body of a dead man popped up in the water beside them.

2

THE BODY APPEARED out of nowhere—a bloated, blotchy mass of human flesh floating facedown, arms and legs splayed like a parachutist in free fall. Only this *thing* hadn't come from the sky. It had emerged from the pond like a whale bursting from the depths of the sea. The boys stood frozen, gaping in horror at the grotesque form.

Collin was the first to react. "Ah-ah-ah!" he cried. He stumbled backward, letting go of the branch, and like a sailor abandoning ship, hurled himself into the pond on the side of the raft away from the floating corpse. He flailed his arms and legs furiously, churning the water but getting nowhere. Then realizing he could stand, he gained his footing and sloshed his way toward shore.

Seth's response was just the opposite. Seeing the body fixed him with fear. He knew what it was, but the reality of it was too much for his brain to process, so it simply shut down. He stood there mindless as a tree stump and as rooted to the spot.

When he finally came to his senses, he felt a mad

desire to follow his friend. "Wait!" he shouted as Collin splashed into the water. But Collin wasn't waiting, and Seth didn't know why *he was*.

He watched Collin thrash around like a drowning victim before coming upright. *He's standing!* The pond wasn't so deep after all.

The sight of Collin slogging toward shore provided the incentive Seth needed, and he jumped too. But he lacked his friend's height and was barely able to keep his face out of the water as he floundered shoreward, slip-sliding with every step on the miry bottom.

Rushing only made things worse. With each incautious stride, his feet would go out from under him. His head would dip under the surface, and panic would set in as he struggled to keep from inhaling water. Then managing to get his feet replanted, he would thrust himself upward and resurface, gasping desperately but more determined than ever to make it to shore.

When at last he dragged himself onto land, he was crying and his chest was heaving. He puked from the brackish water he had swallowed, and from the fear.

Collin sat slumped over on the bank, head between his knees, huffing. Strands of moss garlanded his sopping-wet T-shirt. Dark-brown mud clung to his shoes and splotched the pant legs of his jeans.

Seth glared at him. "Why didn't you wait?"

"For what?"

"For me!" he screamed.

Collin gave no answer.

Seth collapsed onto the bank. He knew what they

had to do, but first he needed to get his wind back and calm his shattered nerves. He spat repeatedly to rid himself of the sour taste of vomit. "We gotta tell someone," he said, wheezing out the words.

"Who?"

"A grown-up."

The boys headed for Seth's house because it was closer. Also, Seth knew that his mother would be home. That morning at breakfast she'd announced her plans to spend the day baking for a fundraiser at the local grange this coming weekend.

Collin, the faster runner, took the lead. By the time Seth scrambled through a hole in the fence around the log compound, Collin was partway across the adjoining meadow. From there the land sloped up to the treed knoll on which sat the Roberson family home—a two-story, wood-framed structure with shutters and a covered front porch with a bench swing hanging from its rafters. Beyond the house were the shop building where Seth's dad did his woodworking, his mother's fenced vegetable garden, and the chicken coop with the wire pen to keep the foxes and raccoons out.

What Seth lacked in speed, he made up for in determination. As Collin neared the house, Seth caught up with him. "Around back," he said in a breathy voice. The back door was closer to the kitchen, where Seth expected to find his mother. What's more, crisis or no crisis, he knew better than to charge in through the front door and track pond sludge through the house. His mother had rules she strictly enforced, and she'd made it quite clear to her children early on what a mudroom was for.

The boys scurried around to the back porch and clambered up the steps, onto the landing. Seth flung open the back door. "Mom! Come quick! Something bad has happened!"

His mother came straightaway, her footsteps clip-clopping down the hallway that led from the kitchen, past the laundry room and mudroom, to the back door. She wore a checkered apron over a flowered sundress. Her shoulder-length red hair was pulled back and netted. In a raised fist, she held a spatula glazed with chocolate frosting. "What is it?" She pulled up short and stared at them. "What happened to you two?"

Fighting for air, Seth could hardly get out any more words. "A body—"

"A body?"

"Floating in the log pond," Collin said. "A dead body."

Seth's mother knitted her brow. "Surely you don't mean a human body."

"Yes—human," Collin said, nodding as animatedly as a bobblehead.

She waved her spatula at them. "You boys wouldn't be making this up, would you? Because if you are . . ."

Seth gulped some air and blew it out. "Mom, we're not making it up."

His mother wasn't convinced. "Because if you are, your dad is going to hear about this. You know what we've told you kids about making up stories."

"Mom—please listen," Seth pleaded, frustrated by his mother's skepticism, though he should have been used to it by now. She demanded a "cross your

heart and hope to die" oath from a child before accepting their word. This was because Seth's seven-year-old sister, Baylie, having a fertile imagination, often told tall tales to garner attention. As if she wasn't fawned over enough, especially by Grandma Claire. But Seth had never felt the need to compete with his sister for the limelight. And even if he had, this wasn't the kind of attention he wanted.

"We're telling the truth, Mrs. Roberson," Collin said. "Honest. There's a dead man floating in the pond."

Seth's mother clamped the hand that held the spatula over her mouth. "Oh dear." When she removed her hand, brown frosting trailed scar-like across her cheek. "I'd better call 911." And she went to do that, but only after making the boys swear "on a stack of Bibles" that they were being truthful.

Seth sat down on the back porch steps, unlaced his sneakers, and pulled them off. He dug his pocket-knife out of his soggy trousers pocket, opened the bigger of its two blades, and began scraping mud from the shoe treads. Collin walked around the backyard, grinding the soles of his sneakers into the grass.

"You can use my knife when I'm done," Seth told him.

"Nah, that's okay," Collin said as he kept grinding—heel, then toe, one foot, then the other—giving rise to smooshed whorls of mud-spiked grass.

Seth felt bad for his friend, because *his* pocket-knife—a spiffy red Swiss Army knife he'd gotten for Christmas from his parents last year—had been stolen a few weeks earlier. It had happened at Beaver

Cove, a sandy-bottomed inlet along Beaver Creek that was a popular swimming hole for both the country kids and the townies. The boys were sure one of the townies had pinched Collin's knife, but they couldn't prove it.

"Don't say anything to my parents," Collin told Seth in a quivering voice after discovering his knife missing. "My dad would skin me alive if he knew."

Seth promised not to say anything. He knew that Collin's dad wouldn't actually skin him alive. But he'd seen the fear in Collin's eyes and knew that it was well founded. Mr. Feeney had a temper and a broad hand he wasn't hesitant to use as a paddle.

The back door of the house opened and Seth's mother filled the doorway. In place of her spatula, she clutched a handset to the cordless house phone. The chocolate scar on her cheek was now a brown smudge, and there was a matching smear on the handset.

"I made the 911 call," she said. "I also called your father, Seth. He's on his way home."

Seth mulled over that development, unsure as to whether it was good news or bad. His dad was a biologist at the local office of Oregon Fish and Wildlife. Seth didn't know how his dad would feel about being called away from work so abruptly. Then again, this situation clearly demanded adult involvement.

"The 911 operator has dispatched a sheriff's deputy to the log pond," his mother said. "He'll want to talk to you boys, and I want your father there when he does." She turned her attention to Collin. "What about *your* dad, Collin?"

Collin stopped grinding. He stood immobile, like a

mechanical toy that had lost battery power. "My dad?" he said, coming back to life. "Uh . . . Dad's felling timber in the hills near Camas Valley. I don't think you can get ahold of him. Poor cell phone service there—that's what he told my mom anyway."

"Okay," Seth's mother said, not pressing him.

Seth knew why. His mother wasn't fond of Mr. Feeney, whom she'd referred to on more than one occasion as "a bit rough around the edges."

"I'll call your mother and let her know what's going on. Meanwhile, you boys use the garden hose to rinse yourselves off." She turned to head back into the house. "How'd *that* happen?" she muttered as she used the tail of her apron to wipe chocolate frosting off the phone.

Seth unwound the backyard garden hose, connected a spray nozzle to its end fitting, and turned the spigot on. When water gushed out, he adjusted it to a jet spray.

"You first," he told Collin.

Collin took a wide-legged, outstretched-arms stance, and Seth began hosing him down.

"Look, I'm a scarecrow," Collin called out, lolling his head to the side and flashing a silly grin.

"You look more like a zombie fresh from the grave."

"*Aaahhhggg*," Collin uttered and took a menacing step toward Seth.

Seth forced him back with a blast of water to the chest. "Stand still."

"That's no fun."

"This isn't supposed to be fun."

Chocolate milk-colored water sluiced down Collin's

pant legs as Seth worked the spray up and down his friend's lower body. "Now turn around."

Collin performed an awkward pirouette. "We'll never get all this crud off," he grumbled.

"No spraying in the face," Seth said when it was Collin's turn to wield the nozzle. But Collin couldn't resist. He laughed as he aimed the flow at Seth's head. Seth saw it coming and turned away. "You're a putz, Feeney."

"I know," Collin said, cackling. He targeted Seth's buttocks. "Bunghole invasion!"

Seth's mom brought them clean clothes and shoes to change into. "I don't think anything of Seth's will fit you, Collin. But here's one of my husband's T-shirts and a pair of his jeans. They'll be baggy and you'll have to roll up the pant legs, but they'll have to do." She handed him a pair of pink sandals. "I think these shoes of mine will fit you well enough." She made a shooing motion. "Now you two go into the garage and change. Leave your dirty clothes there and I'll take care of them."

Seth took the clean clothes without comment. He was more than ready to shed the ones he had on, which clung to his skin like bad memories.

Collin was less enthusiastic. He held the clothes out in front of him, eying them with a wounded look on his face, as if he'd been told to put on a tutu. "Can't I just keep on what I'm wearing?"

Seth's mother jutted her chin. "No, you cannot. My husband will be here soon to pick you boys up. You can't get in his car with those grubby, wet clothes on." She started back toward the house, then paused. "By the way, Collin, I talked to your mother.

She said you're to come straight home as soon as the police are done with you."

"Okay," Collin said, hanging his head.

The boys had just finished changing when the blue Ford Taurus that Seth's dad drove for work came up the gravel drive, trailing a plume of dust. Seth and Collin came out of the garage to meet it. The Taurus skidded to a stop in the driveway, the dust plume enveloping it before settling to the ground.

Seth's dad rolled his window down. "Into the backseat, boys."

Seth's mother came out onto the front porch and hollered, "The deputy said to meet him at the gated entrance to the old log compound off Tilson Road."

"Will do," Seth's dad hollered back.

The boys climbed into the backseat, Collin maneuvering clumsily in his rolled-up baggy jeans, T-shirt that fit him like a sack, and pink sandals. Under other circumstances, Seth would have thought it funny. But there was nothing humorous about discovering a dead body. And now they had to face the police.

3

WHEN THEY ARRIVED at the entrance to the log compound, the sheriff's deputy was already there, sitting in his patrol car parked in front of the gate with the driver's door ajar. Late morning and it was already hot.

Seth's dad pulled in behind the cruiser and shut off the engine.

The deputy got out of his vehicle and walked over to the Taurus. Not the imposing figure Seth had expected, he was in fact rather ordinary looking: medium build, brush-cut blond hair, clean-shaven to apple smoothness. Stripped of the trappings of his profession—khaki-over-army-green uniform, gun belt, and badge—he could have been taken for a school-teacher or a car salesman or a store clerk, or simply someone's dad. But given the situation, Seth couldn't separate the man from his regalia, and what he felt as the officer approached was respect mixed with apprehension.

Seth's dad put his window down.

"I'm Deputy Waller," the officer said, his voice un-expectedly friendly.

"David Roberson."

The two men shook hands through the open window.

"Gate's locked," the deputy said. "McDougal from the mill is on his way to open it. Looks like the access road is overgrown with weeds and vines. I've got a push bumper on my rig, so I'll go first and blaze a trail."

"Suits me."

The deputy glanced into the backseat. "Okay if I talk to the boys?"

"Be my guest. My son, Seth, closest to you, and his friend Collin."

Seth flinched as the window next to him lowered at his dad's push-button command. The deputy's face and upper torso came into view, portrait-like, within the window frame. The gold badge on his chest, a seven-pointed star, flashed arrows of sunlight into the car. Seth had seen the emblem many times, blazoned on the side of the sheriff's depart-ment vehicles that patrolled the county roads. But until now he'd never seen the real thing up close and personal.

"Sounds as if you boys have had quite a morn-ing," Deputy Waller said.

The boys nodded.

"Mind telling me about it?"

Seth looked at Collin, expecting him to speak up.

"Go ahead, son," Seth's dad said. "Tell him what happened."

Seth didn't know where to start. "We . . . uh . . . we built a raft," he said and went on from there. He didn't get far into his story before Collin chimed in with his own details, which was fine with Seth.

"And that's when the body popped up in the water," Collin said with an end-of-the-story flourish.

Seth shuddered as the image of that bloated *thing* resurfaced in his mind. He did his best to push it away, but it was like trying to shoo a ghost.

The deputy's brow hitched. "Must have been a heck of a shock."

"Yessir," the boys replied.

"You boys come to the pond often?"

Seth's mouth went dry. It was a simple question. But if he told the truth, he'd be admitting to trespassing. Beside him, Collin had suddenly gone mute. "In the summer we do," Seth answered. Then, seeking cover, he added, "But it's okay with our parents. Right, Dad?"

Seth's dad, put on the spot, was quick to explain. "We live nearby," he told the deputy. "So does Collin's family. My wife and I wouldn't normally approve of the boys going onto private property. But Southern Oregon Lumber, which still owns the land, hasn't used this log compound for over thirty years. Fact is, I played here as a boy, so it would be hypocritical of me to tell Seth not to. We do, however, caution the boys to be careful and leave if anyone tells them to."

The deputy placed his hands on the window frame and leaned in closer. He eyed the boys in turn. "Anyone ever told you to leave?"

"No, sir," Seth said.

"There's never anybody else around," Collin put in.

"Except . . .," Seth said, prepared to correct his friend.

"Oh yeah," Collin said. "No one except some old man who comes down to the pond to fish."

"And who's that?" the deputy asked.

"Don't know his name," Seth said. "All we know is that he lives up there." He pointed at the wooded hill to the south, where a small house sat on a cut toward the top of the slope. It was the only home on the hill.

The deputy peered up at the house. "How about you, Mr. Roberson? You know the man who lives up there?"

"Not really," Seth's dad said. "I met him once a few years ago when some of his mail was delivered to our house by mistake and I took it up him. He said thanks, and that was it. I haven't had any contact with him since. He's lived up there a long time though—I know that. But he stays to himself."

"Remember his name?"

"Last name's Garber, I think. Don't remember his first name."

The deputy took a pen and notepad from his shirt pocket and jotted down the name. He was about to say something else when a green SUV pulled to a crunching stop behind the Taurus. He tapped the window frame. "Looks like our key is here. Let's go on to the pond and have a look. We'll talk more afterward."

4

THE BOYS BANGED SHOULDERS in the backseat of
the Taurus as they vied for a view out a side window. The car was parked on the high ground above
the pond not far from the old watchman's shack,
overlooking the spot where the boys had launched
their makeshift raft. The deputy's cruiser, its push
bumper having done its job, was parked in front of
them. Behind them sat a lime-green Jeep Cherokee
with a Southern Oregon Lumber Company logo on
the side.

"I wish we could get closer," Collin said, his head
and nearly half his body out the window.

Seth squeezed into the remaining space. "Dad said
to stay in the car."

"But it's hot in here and we can't hear what
they're saying."

"Then best we keep quiet and listen harder."

But they were too far away to hear anything except the honking of geese flying overhead and the
revving of a chainsaw in the distance.

Seth kept his vision trained on the sheriff's deputy. The man stood on the bank of the pond, holding a pair of binoculars up to his eyes. Beside him stood Seth's dad and Mr. McDougal, a manager at Southern Oregon Lumber.

"He's looking for the body," Collin said. "He wants to make sure we're telling the truth."

"Of course we're telling the truth," Seth said, though secretly he feared that maybe they had only imagined it was a human body they'd seen. What if it was just some dead animal? A beaver or a nutria. *How embarrassing that would be!*

The three men lingered on the bank, gazing out over the water. They talked among themselves, their voices muffled by the warm breeze fanning the valley. The deputy pointed out to the middle of the pond, where the boys' raft floated as hapless as an empty lifeboat. The men took turns looking through the binoculars. Then they walked back up the slope.

Seth's dad came over to the Taurus and opened a back door. The boys scrambled out and stood in the bright sunlight. To Seth, it didn't feel much cooler outside the car than in, but at least he didn't have to compete with Collin for breathing space.

"Thanks, boys, for waiting in the car," Deputy Waller said.

"Did you see the body?" Collin blurted.

The deputy shook his head. "No. But that's not surprising. A floating body is difficult to spot from a distance. Also, it could have drifted away from the raft. We need a closer look."

"There's a body out there, all right," Collin said. "I know a dead body when I see one."

Seth wasn't so sure now that *he would.*

"I don't doubt your story," Waller said. "But since I'm not inclined to slog out into that mud trough to conduct a search, I've called for reinforcements. They should be here soon. In the meantime, let's talk more about what happened here."

The deputy had the boys tell their story again. This time he took notes, occasionally interjecting a question, but mostly letting them talk as before. They had nearly come to the end of their story for a second time when Mr. McDougal stepped up.

"Sorry to interrupt, but the reinforcements have arrived." He nodded toward a mud-spattered pickup truck with two men in the cab, approaching on the weed-infested access road. The truck towed a flatbed trailer carrying a red inflatable raft with a rear-mounted outboard motor. Lettering on the side of the raft read DOUGLAS COUNTY SHERIFF'S SEARCH AND RESCUE.

"Just the help we need," the deputy said. He signaled for the truck's driver to pull around the line of cars to a location closer to the bank.

"Back in the car, boys," Seth's dad said.

"But *Daaad . . .*"

"In."

Grudgingly the boys returned to their roles as backseat observers.

Seth sized up the new arrivals as they exited their truck. They were dressed in well-worn jeans, faded T-shirts, and baseball caps. One had a beard with blotches of gray in it and looked considerably older than the other. The younger one had long, shaggy sideburns and a stubbled chin.

"These guys don't look all that professional," Seth said. "In fact, they look like fishermen who missed the turnoff to the river."

"They're probably volunteers," Collin said. "My uncle volunteers on the four-wheel-drive search team. He says that most of the county's search and rescue team members are volunteers. They don't have to *look* professional. They just have to know what they're doing."

These men clearly did.

After a brief conversation with Deputy Waller, the new arrivals accompanied the other men to the edge of the pond. More gesturing and talking took place, none of which the boys could make out. Then the two search and rescue men returned to their truck while the others waited along the shore.

The boys watched with anticipation as the men retrieved items from a storage box in the bed of the truck. The older man put on an orange life vest and a yellow helmet. The younger man slid his legs into chest-high waders like the ones fly fishermen wear. He too donned a life vest and a helmet. Then they went to the trailer, unlashed the raft, and slid it onto the ground. They were close enough now for the boys to overhear their conversation.

"Too shallow and too many hidden hazards to risk motoring out," the older man said. He locked the motor in place with its propeller above the waterline. "Besides, you love to paddle."

The younger man feigned a smile. "It's what I live for."

They grasped ties on opposite sides of the raft and began hauling it toward the bank. After only a few steps, they halted and turned to face the entrance to the pond.

"Someone else is coming," Collin said, wriggling around to see.

Seth peered out the Taurus's back window. Another pickup truck approached—this one cleaner, newer, and with a lightbar on top. As it pulled in beside the search and rescue vehicle, he noted the gold sheriff's star on its side. Below the star were stenciled the words MARINE PATROL.

The driver's door swung open and a uniformed officer stepped out. He was short and wiry and ruddy faced. He wore dark sunglasses and a baseball cap that struggled to contain a mop of curly brown hair.

"Better late than never," the older search and rescue team member said.

"Hey, I was halfway to Lemolo Lake when I got the call," the marine patrol officer said. "This rig doesn't have wings." He gestured toward the pond. "What do we have here?"

"Report of a floater. Just heading out to take a look."

"Three's company," the marine patrol officer said. He got a life vest out of his truck and shrugged it on. He took hold of a tie at the bow of the raft. "Let's do it."

The three men hefted the raft down the slope to the shoreline, where the other men waited. More talking and pointing ensued among the group, which now numbered six. Then the three men in life vests slid the raft into the water and, one at a time, stepped in. The two search and rescue team members, seating themselves opposite one another on the raft's bloated side tubes, took up paddles and dipped them into the water.

Seth felt a jolt of anxiety as he watched the raft move away from shore. "What if they can't find the body?"

"They'll find it," Collin said, as if he knew something nobody else did.

The boys poked their heads out the car window as far as they could and watched the scene unfold. Even without using the motor, the search and rescue team took little time reaching the boys' homemade raft.

From his position on the bank, Deputy Waller cupped his hands around his mouth and hollered out across the water, "See anything?"

The marine patrol officer made a thumbs-down gesture.

Seth's heart was pounding now. "What if the body sank? What if it got stuck on the bottom again?" *What if there never was a body?*

"They'll find it," Collin repeated.

With deliberate strokes, the paddlers circled the rescue boat around the boys' abandoned raft. Apparently finding nothing, they widened the search circle. They were about to complete a second loop when the marine patrol officer pointed off to the side. The paddlers headed the boat in that direction. The marine patrol officer leaned over and peered into the water. He raised an arm and made a circle in the air.

"They found it!" Collin said. "I knew they would."

But Seth wasn't convinced that the "it" they'd found was in fact a human body. And he didn't know

27

whether to wish that it was or it wasn't. If it *was* human, then someone had lost their life, and how awful that would be. But if it wasn't human, he would feel awfully foolish for causing such a fuss.

Shielding his eyes from the sunlight glimmering off the pond, he kept his gaze on the marine patrol officer. The officer reached down into the boat and came up with something in his hands. He drew back his arm and cast the something into the water.

Seth could see it now—a red ball, like an oversized fishing bobber, floating off to the side of the search and rescue raft.

"Red ball marks the spot," Collin said, as if referring to an *X* on a treasure map.

What happened next surprised the boys. The paddlers began maneuvering their craft toward shore.

"Why are they coming back and leaving the body out there?" Seth wondered aloud, doubt still plaguing his thinking. *Is the dead thing human or isn't it?*

For once, Collin had no answer.

The next person to arrive on the scene brought the answer with him.

5

THE MAN ARRIVED in an unmarked white crew cab pickup with a windowless canopy. He stepped out of the truck with a sense of purpose. A brawny man with close-cropped hair, he wore tan trousers and a black polo shirt.

The men already on the scene, having regrouped on the high ground above the pond, greeted the newcomer as if pleased to see him, each shaking hands with him in turn.

"Who's this guy?" Collin muttered. "He's not wearing a uniform and he doesn't drive a police car. But he's got a badge on his belt."

Seth had noticed the badge as well. "I don't know," he said. "But he must be someone important."

After the round of greetings, the newcomer returned to his truck. He opened a storage bin on the side of the truck and brought out a tote bag. He pulled out a pair of dark blue coveralls and tugged them on over his street clothes. After taking off his shoes, he slid his stocking feet into tall rubber boots. He removed a camera from its carrying case and hung it by a strap around his neck. Then he took a separate tote from the truck and rejoined the other men.

It was then that the boys were able to read the words on the back of the man's coveralls: MEDICAL EXAMINER.

"He's someone important, all right," Collin said. "And that's no ordinary pickup he's driving. That's a body wagon!"

Seth suddenly felt queasy. *It really is a human body out there in the pond!*

"Now we'll get some action," Collin said with hand-rubbing enthusiasm, as if his panic-stricken leap into the pond at the sight of the floating corpse had never happened.

Lacking his friend's bravado, Seth looked on with misgiving as the cluster of men trekked down the embankment to the water's edge and the waiting search and rescue raft. The medical examiner and the marine patrol officer boarded the craft. The two search and rescue team members joined them. Resuming their role as paddlers, they propelled the raft out to the bobbing red marker.

Seth squinted, straining to see what was happening out on the pond. The medical examiner was leaning over the side of the rescue boat with his camera to his face. "He's taking pictures."

Collin let out a ghoulish laugh. "Not pretty ones— you can be sure of that."

Seth could only imagine. He gave his head a brisk shake. He didn't *want* to imagine.

The medical examiner put his camera away. From his tote, he retrieved a bright yellow bundle. The boys couldn't tell what it was at first. Then he unfolded it, and Seth saw that it was a big mesh bag.

The younger search and rescue team member, obviously aware of his role in this ongoing drama, took possession of the bag. He tightened the shoulder straps on his waders, swung his legs over the side of the raft, and slid into the water.

Seth sensed what was about to happen and wasn't sure he wanted to watch, but he couldn't tear his eyes away.

With the mesh bag unfurled, the man in the water folded back its top flap. Slowly, carefully—as if dealing with a breakable object—he slipped the bag up and around the body until it was fully contained. Then he zipped the flap closed, sealing the body inside.

"Just like netting a big fish," Collin said, his voice pitchy with excitement—excitement that Seth didn't share.

The medical examiner reached out and gripped a handhold at the top of the bag. Then the man in the water, maintaining a grasp on the trailing end of the bag, walked along behind the raft as his fellow team member and the marine patrol officer paddled it slowly to shore.

Seth's heartbeat drummed in his ears. *Who could it be in that bag?* He recalled the story of the young girl who'd drowned in the pond. But that had happened years ago, before the log compound was closed to the public. Nowadays the fence and the no trespassing signs kept everyone out—everyone that is except for him and Collin . . . and . . . "When's the last time we saw that old fisherman here at the pond?"

"Come to think of it," Collin said, "it's been several days." His eyes widened. "You think it could be him in the bag?"

Seth felt an unwelcome chill, like a cold hand on the back of his neck. "I hope not."

"Well, whoever it is, he's deader than a doornail now. Food for worms. Stiffer than a peppermint stick—"

"Oh, zip it and be serious for once."

"I *am* being serious," Collin said.

Seth sighed because he knew that, absurdly, this was true.

The men waiting on the shore backed away as the rescue team members carefully lifted the body out of the pond and placed it on the bank. Water drained from the mesh bag and ran downhill. Seth's dad clamped a hand over his nose and mouth. The man from the mill took a handkerchief from his pocket and covered his face. It didn't take long for the boys to understand why.

"Pee-yew," Collin said, getting a whiff of the foul odor wafting up the slope. "Smells worse than a pit toilet."

The stench reminded Seth of the time the compressor on the chest freezer in their garage went out and they didn't discover it until three days later. When his dad opened the freezer, the stink from all the spoiled meat made Seth feel like throwing up. He would have too, if he hadn't run outside and taken big gulps of fresh air.

On the bank below, the action continued to play

out. While the other men kept their distance, the medical examiner unzipped the mesh bag's flap and turned it back. Taking up his camera again, he snapped pictures of the body from various angles. Then he got some gloves out of his tote and pulled them on. He knelt over the corpse.

"He's frisking a dead man," Collin said, "and it looks like he found something."

The medical examiner held out an object. Deputy Waller approached and scrutinized the object without touching it. The two men exchanged words. The medical examiner slipped the object into a clear plastic bag, which he placed in his tote.

He motioned for Seth's dad and Mr. McDougal to come closer. The two men inched forward, hovered over the corpse momentarily, then tucked their chins to their chests and backed away.

Seth swallowed a lump of emotion now as he watched the medical examiner remove a black bundle from his tote. There was no question in his mind this time what the bundle was. The medical examiner spread out the large black bag, unzipped its flap, and turned it back.

Assisted by the marine patrol officer, the medical examiner slipped the black bag up and around the yellow mesh bag, sheathing its contents, and zipped it closed. Then he seized his tote and trudged up the slope along with Deputy Waller. The marine patrol officer, Seth's dad, and Mr. McDougal followed, while the other two men stayed with the body.

"Let me know what you find in your search of the area," the medical examiner said to the deputy.

"Will do," Waller replied as the medical examiner

B. K. Mayo

headed back to his truck, accompanied by the marine patrol officer.

"You need me for anything else?" Mr. McDougal asked the deputy.

"I don't think so, Tom. Thanks for coming out and opening the gate for us. I'll lock up when we're done here. And I'll keep you posted on the medical examiner's findings."

"I'd appreciate it," McDougal said.

"What about the boys?" Seth's dad asked.

"I'd like a last word with them," the deputy said, "if you don't mind."

Even as he listened to these exchanges, Seth continued tracking the movements of the medical examiner. Arriving back at his truck, he stowed his tote in the storage bin. Then he went to the rear of the truck, swung open its big bay door, and withdrew a wheeled cot. Now, with the assistance of the marine patrol officer, he was wheeling the cot down the embankment.

Seth's dad approached the Taurus.

"Who is it, Mr. Roberson?" Collin called out the window. "Who's the dead person?"

"Is it someone you know, Dad?" Seth asked.

"Hold your questions for the deputy, boys." He opened the car door and the boys bailed out as Deputy Waller drew near.

"First of all," Waller said. "I want to commend you boys on the way you handled yourselves today. You've been a big help."

Hearing this pleased Seth, but Collin's focus was obviously elsewhere. He pointed at the bundle on the bank. "Who's in the bag?"

34

The deputy glanced down the slope. "I reckon you boys have earned the right to know. The medical examiner will have to confirm identification. But based on a driver's license found on the body, the deceased appears to be the fisherman you boys were telling me about, one Henry Garber."

Seth's stomach lurched. "Are you sure?"

"I'm afraid so, son," his dad said.

Deputy Waller gazed up at the wooded hill to the south. "You say he lived in that house up there?"

The boys nodded.

"Anyone live with him?"

The boys didn't know.

"I believe he lived alone," Seth's dad said.

"Did he have any kin around here?"

Seth's dad shrugged. "That I wouldn't know."

"Okay, we'll check out the house." The deputy took out his pad and scrawled a note. "Now, boys, when Mr. Garber came to the pond, how did he get here? According to Mr. McDougal, the gate to the compound is kept locked. Did Garber park a vehicle outside the gate and hike the fence?"

"We never saw a vehicle," Collin said.

"He would just appear," Seth said, "carrying a fishing rod and a tackle box. Him and his dog."

"Just appear?" the deputy said. He looked vaguely puzzled, then moved on. "Did he fish from the shore or from a boat?"

"From an old rowboat he kept stashed in the brush along the shore," Seth said.

"Ever see anyone with him?"

"Nah," Collin said, "he was always by himself."

"Except for the dog," Seth added. "He was never

without his dog."

"What kind of dog?"

"A scraggly mutt," Collin said.

"Some kind of terrier, I think," Seth said. He'd paid attention to the dog even though seeing it always saddened him because it made him think of his own dog that had died. "It's got shaggy gray hair and a bearded muzzle."

"I'll let my guys know to keep an eye out for the dog," the deputy said. "Now tell me, boys, when Mr. Garber was down at the pond, did you ever talk to him?"

Seth was quick to answer. "No, sir. My grandmother said we should keep our distance from him because he wasn't right in the head."

"Your grandmother knew the man?"

"I guess so."

The deputy turned to Seth's dad. "Is that right, Mr. Roberson?"

"If it is, then it's news to me," Seth's dad said. "But I wouldn't be surprised if that were the case. My parents lived in this valley for a long time. In fact, they lived in the house we live in now. It's the house I grew up in. When my wife and I got married, my parents gave us the house and moved into a new one they had built nearby. Mom continued living there by herself after my dad died. Then a year or so ago, she moved into town. So Mom knows a lot of people in this neighborhood. It's entirely possible that she was acquainted with this fellow. But you'd have to ask her."

The deputy scribbled some more on his pad.

By this time, the medical examiner and his helpers

had conveyed Henry Garber's body up the embankment and over to the medical examiner's truck. Seth's eyes were drawn to the action there.

The truck's bay door gaped open. The men lifted the wheeled cot with its freight. Sunlight glinted off the human-shaped contours of the black bag as they slid the cot into the bed of the truck. The medical examiner slammed the door shut.

Seth felt a shiver run down his spine. *Body wagon*, Collin had called the truck, and he'd been right.

"Isn't that right, Seth?" Collin said.

Seth looked at his friend. "What?"

"We never talked to that old man, but he spoke to us once."

"Uh . . . oh . . . right," Seth said, recalling the one and only time the man had spoken to them.

"What did he say?" the deputy asked.

Collin kicked at the ground with a floppy pink sandal. "He said we should try not to drown ourselves in the pond."

The deputy's eyebrows arched. "Looks like he should have followed his own advice."

6

WHEN SETH AND HIS DAD dropped Collin off at his house, Collin's mother came out onto the front porch and stood with her arms crossed, looking at odds with the world. "Nice shoes," she said as Collin, head down, slunk past her and disappeared into the house.

Seth waved at Mrs. Feeney. She did not wave back.

"I have to go back to the office," Seth's dad said on their way home. "You stay around the house for the rest of the day. We'll talk when I get home. I'll try to get off early."

Seth always felt uneasy whenever one of his parents said, "We'll talk later." He never knew what to expect. It was like when Collin said to him, "Close your eyes—I have a surprise for you." A blind surprise came in one of two opposing flavors: fright or delight. Seth didn't like having to guess which one he was about to receive.

When he got home, the whole house had the warm, sweet smell of a bakery. Pies and cakes on cooling racks decked the kitchen counter. What should have been a pleasant aroma soured in Seth's throat.

"All done with the cakes, and the last of the pies are in the oven," his mother announced with satisfaction. She wiped her hands on an apron smudged with frosting and traces of pie filling.

Seth felt very tired. "That's good, Mom."

His mother came to him and enveloped him in a hug, her neck sweaty against his cheek. "You okay? Your dad called and told me what they found."

Seth took a ragged breath. "You mean *who*?"

"Yes. And I'm so sorry you boys had to be the ones to find him. That's so awful."

"I'm fine, Mom. Just tired."

"You must be hungry. Can I fix you something?"

"I don't think I could eat anything right now."

His mother kissed him on the forehead. "All right, but I'm here for you if you need me."

"I know, Mom. Thanks. But I'm okay, really."

He went upstairs to his room and flopped onto his bed. Despite his claim, he wasn't okay. The morning's events had left him shaken and confused. Try as he might, he couldn't rid his mind of the image of Mr. Garber's bloated body popping up in the water alongside the raft. The terror of that moment, and of his panicked response, lingered like a nightmare from which he was unable to awaken.

What had happened to the old man? How had he died? And when? As Seth lay there pondering these questions, a deep sadness came over him and he began to cry. Angrily, he swiped at the tears with the back of his hand. *Why am I crying? What was that old man to me?* He didn't even know Henry Garber, had never been close enough to him to look him in the eye or shake his hand. The old man could have been a ghost, for all he knew.

Yet Seth's sorrow was undeniable. He was seized by a keen sense of loss, as if he'd been given a precious gift, only to have it suddenly taken away. He'd seen the old man so often—sitting in his rowboat out on the pond, fishing rod in hand, dog at his side—that, unknown to Seth, the man had become a fixture in the landscape of his life. There was comfort in such familiarity. And as he now knew, there was pain in its loss.

SETH DIDN'T REALIZE he'd fallen asleep until he woke up to the sound of his father's voice downstairs and another familiar voice. He sat up in bed and listened hard. It sounded like the officer from the pond. What was his name? Waller. That was it, Deputy Waller.

He got up groggily and stumbled out of his room and down the second-floor hallway to the stairwell.

"I assumed you'd want to know what we found out," he heard the deputy say.

Seth shambled down the stairs and into the living room. The deputy sat in his dad's recliner, his gun belt askew. His mom and dad sat together on the sofa.

"There's Rip Van Winkle," his dad said. "I thought we were going to have to wake you for dinner."

His mom patted the vacant space beside her. "Come here, honey."

Seth rubbed his eyes. "I'm thirsty."

"I'll get you some juice," his mother said. She rose

and went into the kitchen.

Seth glanced around as he sank onto the sofa. "Where's Baylie?"

"At a birthday party, I think your mother said."

Seth's mother returned with some apple juice. He gulped it in one tip of the glass.

"Deputy Waller was about to fill us in on the results of his investigation so far," his dad said.

"Can I hear too?" Seth asked.

"If it's okay with your parents," the deputy said.

Seth's dad raked his fingers through his hair. "I don't see why not. I think he's earned the right to be kept in the loop."

"All right, then," Waller said, leaning forward in his chair. "After you left the pond, I brought in additional deputies to search the area while I and another officer went up and checked out Mr. Garber's house. Here's what we know so far." He referred to his notepad. "The deceased's full name is Henry Thomas Garber. He resided at 480 Fir Hill Road. It appears that he lived alone. As far as next of kin, we didn't find anything to help us out there—no address book, no personal letters, no family photos, no Christmas or birthday cards. None of the things you'd normally use to trace family ties.

"We did find discharge papers indicating he was a veteran, so we'll have the local Veterans Affairs office search their records. That's probably our best bet for locating next of kin."

"What about his dog?" Seth asked. The way he saw it, the dog was the man's true companion. It might not be able to talk, but you can learn a lot about people from their pets.

The deputy shook his head. "We didn't find a dog. He evidently had one though. There was a bag of dog chow in a cabinet and food and water bowls on the kitchen floor."

"The dog's got to be around somewhere," Seth said. "We never saw the old man without his dog. Even when he was out in his boat, the dog was always with him."

"The boat we found," the deputy said. "The men searching the area around the pond came across an aluminum rowboat floating among some reeds along the east bank. It was unmoored and appeared to have drifted there. It was beat up but watertight. It had some fishing gear in it that we assume belonged to Garber."

"Hmm," Seth's dad said. "Is it possible that Mr. Garber went out fishing and accidentally fell out of his boat and drowned? Had a medical emergency, perhaps? Then the boat drifted to shore?"

"That's conceivable," Deputy Waller said. "We'll be examining all possibilities. But it's too early in our investigation to draw any conclusions." He flipped to another page in his notepad. "One other thing— while searching the perimeter of the pond, we found the spot where Garber had launched his boat. There were two sets of footprints in the mud along the shore. One set of footprints matched Garber's boots. The other set didn't. Different size and sole pattern."

"So someone else—" Seth's dad turned to him. His eyes narrowed. "Did you boys mess with Garber's boat?"

Seth shook his head. "No, sir," he said, feeling guilty for something he hadn't done. "Mr. Garber always hid his boat in the rushes when he wasn't using it. I figured it was because he knew nobody was supposed to be fishing in the pond. Collin and I never went near the old man's boat."

Much to Seth's relief, the deputy backed him up. "I can ease your mind on that question, Mr. Roberson. We've already determined that the footprints don't belong to the boys. They were made by smooth-soled shoes—probably dress shoes—not by the kind of athletic shoes the boys were wearing, or the boots Garber had on."

"Some other person was at the pond, then, around the time of Mr. Garber's death," Seth's dad said.

Waller drummed his pen against his notepad. "Looks like." He glanced at Seth. "Did you boys see anyone else at the pond over the last several days?"

"No," Seth said. "Like we told you, the only other person we ever saw there was Mr. Garber." Then a thought that turned into a question had his heart beating faster. "You think Mr. Garber could have been—" But the word was too weighty to come out of his mouth.

"Murdered?" the deputy said.

Seth nodded.

The deputy gave a noncommittal shrug. "Foul play is a possibility. But as I said, it's too soon to say. I can tell you this much though. I spoke with the medical examiner by phone before coming here. His initial examination of the body revealed no signs of physical trauma—no cuts, bruises, or abrasions— that would indicate a struggle. Although this doesn't rule out foul play, it does make it less likely.

"Furthermore, people who die on land and are then immersed in water don't sink—unless they're weighted, that is. Drowning victims sink when their lungs become saturated with water. Then they rise to the surface as gases form within their body tissue. This can take a couple of days to a week or longer, depending on the temperature and depth of the water. Based on the condition of Mr. Garber's body— taking into account it was found in warm, shallow water, which accelerates the creation of gases—the medical examiner estimates it was in the pond no more than a few days.

"Again, none of this is conclusive as to cause of death. That determination will be made only after the medical examiner has completed examining the body and we've finished investigating the circumstances surrounding the death. But for the time being, I suggest you boys be extra cautious anytime you go down to the pond."

Seth's mother, who'd been quiet until then, said, "You don't have to worry about that, Officer. That pond is off-limits to the boys as of this minute."

"Mom . . ."

"Now, Laura," Seth's dad said, "let's not jump to conclusions here. The man could simply have had a heart attack and tumbled into the water by accident."

Seth's mother straightened her shoulders. "Or, we could have a killer on the loose. You don't know. I'm just glad your mother isn't here right now."

Seth's dad looked puzzled. "Why do you say that?"

"I'm not sure why," she shot back. "But there was something about that old man that bothered Claire, that made her tense up at any mention of him. And

44

now with his suspicious death . . ."

"Where is your mother, Mr. Roberson?" Deputy Waller asked. "I believe you said she lives in town now?"

"Yes, she has an apartment in a fifty-five-plus community, but she's in Minnesota at the moment, visiting her sister."

The deputy nodded. "Well, it sounds as if I ought to speak with her. Can I get her address and phone number from you?"

"Certainly."

The deputy copied the information onto his notepad as Seth's dad recited it. "I guess that's about it for now," he said and stood up. "As soon as I have something more definitive on cause of death, I'll let you folks know."

Seth's dad accompanied the deputy to his car.

Seth went back to his room, taking with him the cordless phone from the den. He closed the door and called Collin. "That deputy came to our house," he said.

"What did he want?"

Seth told him everything Waller had said, including the news of the footprints discovered on the bank of the pond that weren't theirs or Henry Garber's.

"Who'd want to kill that old man?" Collin said.

"They're not saying he was killed—only that someone else was there."

"Sounds suspicious, though."

"Yeah," Seth said. "And now my mom says the pond is off-limits."

"That sucks, and not through a straw."

It was one of Collin's favorite expressions. Seth thought it was silly, but this time he had to agree with his friend. "Big time," he said.

Shortly before dinner, Baylie came home from the birthday party hyped-up on ice cream and birthday cake. She didn't want any supper, and Seth wasn't hungry either, even though he'd missed lunch. His mom made them both sit at the dinner table anyway. She put food on their plates and told them to eat some of it.

Seth ate a few bites of chicken and mashed potatoes. Baylie shuffled food around on her plate with her fork while kicking Seth's chair and chattering about the birthday party.

"May I be excused?" he said.

"You don't want any dessert?" his mother asked.

"No thanks."

"I want dessert," Baylie said.

"Not a chance," their mother said.

"Daddy . . ."

"You heard your mother, Baylie. Now eat what's on your plate."

"I don't want what's on my plate."

"Eat it anyway—at least some of it."

Seth slipped away, not wanting to witness another battle of wills between Baylie and his parents.

He had trouble going to sleep that night. He had too little on his stomach and too much on his mind. When at last he did drift off, he dreamed about the dead man in the pond. Mr. Garber's body floated facedown in the water, fish swimming around it, nibbling on the ears, or what was left of them—

shredded flesh dangling from veins of blue-white cartilage. Then the body heaved and flipped over onto its back, and Seth saw that the eyeballs had been eaten away as well, leaving only bloody sockets.

He woke up crying. But he forced himself to cry quietly because he didn't want to wake up his mom and dad, or Baylie. He didn't want anyone thinking he was a baby. He was eleven years old, more than half grown. He wasn't a man, but he was on his way to becoming one. He didn't want to give anyone a reason to believe otherwise.

Besides, he was sure that Collin wasn't having bad dreams. Collin was stronger than that. Seth wanted to be strong too. But he didn't want to have the bad dream anymore either. So he stayed awake as much as he could, and when finally the soft glow of first light filtered through his bedroom window curtains, he was glad of it.

7

SETH SIGHTED DOWN THE BARREL of his air rifle, drew a bead, and squeezed off a shot. He wasn't surprised when he missed his target, a tin can sitting on a log about forty feet away.

"Let me show you how it's done," Collin said, reaching for the gun. He gave the rifle's lever a couple of pumps, pressed its buttstock against his shoulder, and took aim. A loud pop was closely followed by the familiar clink of a tin can biting the dust.

The boys were in the field between Seth's house and the old log compound. For Seth, the morning had crept by at a caterpillar's pace. He'd finished his chores before the sun had burned away the morning mist. With nothing better to do, he'd gone back to his room and built a few electrical projects with his Snap Circuits kit. But he'd built the same ones several times before and soon lost interest.

He checked his watch frequently, anxious to call Collin. But Collin's mother didn't like anyone calling early in the day. "Mornings are her quiet time," Collin had told him. "Best not to disturb her before nine o'clock." A hitch in his voice hinted at the adverse consequences of doing just that.

Feeling at loose ends, Seth went downstairs and wandered aimlessly through the house.

"Looking for something?" his mother asked.

Seth was baffled by the question. Was he looking for something? He didn't think so. He tapped his watch, thinking it must have been losing minutes. "What time is it?"

"Half past eight."

He grumbled and went back up to his room.

At nine o'clock sharp, he called Collin to see if he could come over.

"I gotta finish cleaning my room first."

Seth rolled his eyes. Collin's bedroom was always a mess. It resembled a debris field in the aftermath of a tornado. "Shove everything into the closet," he told his friend.

"My closet isn't big enough."

An hour later, when Collin showed up, the boys promptly headed outside with Seth's air rifle and a canister of BBs.

"Stay away from the pond," his mother reminded him.

"I know, Mom. I know." Did she think he hadn't heard her the first five times?

Collin passed the air rifle back to Seth.

The boys had lined up tin cans on the trunk of a big oak tree that had blown over in a windstorm several years ago. After stepping back twenty paces, they took turns shooting at the cans. As with everything they did, Collin was more proficient. He scored a hit on nearly every shot, while Seth was lucky to hit one in five.

At first it bothered Seth that Collin was better than him at almost everything. But not anymore. And his friend never rubbed it in. "You're smart," Collin told him once. "When you're smart, you don't have to be good at anything."

Seth wasn't sure how to take the comment, but it made him feel better anyway. He stopped trying to compete with Collin at everything and concentrated on just having fun at whatever they were doing— whether it was tossing a Frisbee, playing games on the Xbox 360, or shooting at tin cans.

And it was true that he did better in school than Collin. They'd been schoolmates ever since first grade, after Collin had been held back a year, and in the fall would start middle school together. His report cards were always better than Collin's, but Seth never rubbed that in.

He took a shooting stance and let off another shot. "At least I hit the log," he said lightheartedly. He handed the gun to Collin.

"I wish we could go down to the pond," Collin said, casting a yearning look in that direction. "I'd rather shoot at frogs."

"Mom says *no way*. And when she makes up her mind about something, even my dad knows to back off. This whole thing has her freaked out. The pond is definitely off-limits."

Collin pumped some air into the rifle's compression chamber. But instead of aiming at the lineup of cans, he pointed the gun at a nearby standing oak tree and pulled the trigger. The rifle went *pop!* Birds scattered.

Seth snatched the gun from his friend. "Don't shoot at the birds. I don't like you shooting at birds."

"Frogs, birds—what's the difference?" Collin said.

"I don't like you shooting at frogs either."

"You don't like me shooting at anything that moves."

"That's not true. I don't care if you shoot at spiders." Seth did not like spiders!

Collin scoffed. "Yeah, sure. Who can hit a spider with a BB gun? You'd need a bazooka." His face lit up. "Say!—now that would be fun, shooting spiders with a bazooka." He hoisted a make-believe bazooka onto his shoulder and aimed it at the ground. "*Kaboom!* Watch those spiders scatter!" He pointed it at the tree.

Seth gave him a nudge. "Not at the birds."

"Okay," Collin said, putting away his imaginary bazooka. His shoulders slumped. "Are you *positive* we can't go down to the pond?"

"I'm positive," Seth said. He held out the air rifle. "Here—it's still your turn. Pretend the cans are enemy soldiers coming over the ridge."

Collin's face brightened. "Yes, I'll single-handedly save the nation." He shouldered the rifle and took aim.

"Hold it," Seth said in a hushed voice before Collin could get off a shot.

Collin lowered the gun. "What?"

Seth pointed into the distance, toward the fence bordering the log compound. "Mr. Garber's dog."

"Where?"

Seth continued pointing. "There—in the tall grass just inside the fence line."

"I don't see anything."

"It's Garber's dog, I tell you."

Collin took a step in that direction. "Only one way to find out."

Seth caught him by the arm. "Go slow and stay low. I don't want to scare him off."

Crouching, the boys crept forward, a high tide of wheat grass helping to screen their advance. When they got to the downed tree with the cans on it, they ducked in behind it. "See him now?" Seth said, peering over the log.

"I see a dog. You sure it's the old man's dog?"

Seth was sure.

"What do you want to do?" Collin asked.

Seth didn't know. If they rushed the dog, it was sure to run. "Let's keep going, but at a crawl. Head for those bushes up there. That should give us some cover."

It wasn't cover enough. Before they'd advanced more than a few yards, crabbing on their hands and knees, the dog took off running. The boys sprang to their feet and raced after it. But by the time they reached the fence line, the dog had disappeared into the sheltering brush.

"See which way it went?" Seth asked breathlessly.

"That way, I think," Collin said, pointing south. "But it's long gone now. And we can't go after it without crossing the fence."

"We can't cross the fence."

"That's it, then."

Seth scanned the brushy landscape south of the pond, his eyes tracing a southbound course the dog might have taken. This assumed path led him to the base of the wooded hill with the lone clearing on its north-facing slope. The sun had yet to rise high enough to dispel the shadows veiling the small house snugged into the hillside—Henry Garber's house.

Seth smiled as a notion came to him as clearly as if a voice had whispered it in his ear. "Maybe not," he said.

"What do you mean?" Collin asked.

"Where would a frightened dog go?"

Collin's face took on that familiar pained look that meant his mind was hard at work. Then his eyes shone as if a light bulb had come on behind them. "Home."

Seth felt his first ripple of excitement of the day. "Mom said the pond was off-limits. She didn't say . . ."

8

THE BOYS HUSTLED BACK to Seth's house with renewed prospects for the day. Seth stowed his air rifle in the corner of his bedroom closet where he always kept it, in accordance with his mother's maxim "a place for everything and everything in its place."

They found her downstairs in the den, bent over her sewing machine, stitching a patch onto Baylie's Brownie vest. "Mom, we're going over to Collin's house for a while, if that's okay with you."

Her eyebrows shot up. "As long as you . . ."

". . . stay away from the pond," the boys chanted in unison, and headed back outside.

Seth hadn't lied to his mother, he told himself. They *were* going to Collin's house; they were just taking a shortcut. Seth lived in the vale west of the hillside on which Mr. Garber's house stood, while Collin lived on flatland to the east. A gravel road that accessed both their homes ran around the base of the slope, but the shortest route to Collin's house—one they'd never taken before—was over the hill, through Garber's property, where Seth was certain they'd find the old man's dog.

The boys cut diagonally across the field to the gravel road and then followed it to a spot they reckoned was directly below Garber's house. There they jumped across a drainage ditch and headed up the slope.

It was slow going. The hillside was steep and densely forested. Conifer trees—fir, pine, and cedar —brushed shoulders with their leafy counter-parts, oak and madrone. A canopy of foliage blocked out the sky. It was as if the boys had entered another world. Day abruptly became twilight. The penetrating warmth of the sun gave way to cool damp air. The smell of mown hay that permeated the valley was replaced by the pungent odor of resin and the decaying duff of the forest floor.

Collin led the way as the boys negotiated an obstacle course of tree trunks and low-hanging branches. Unable to see beyond the next picket line of trees, they used the uphill grade as their compass.

Seth was fighting for breath by the time they approached the clearing where Mr. Garber's house stood, by now partially bathed in sunlight. He halted as he rounded the scaly trunk of a big cedar tree. "Hold on," he called out to Collin.

Collin backtracked. "What's up?"

"I don't want to rush in and scare the dog away again."

"I'll tiptoe, then," Collin said and began skulking like a cartoon character toward the clearing.

"Just stay put a second, will you?"

Seth scanned the scene up ahead. An older model pickup truck sat in a gravel driveway in front of a detached garage. The house itself was small and boxy. Its lone front window, winking with reflected sunlight, stood out like the eye of a cyclops. Its front door was sheltered by a gable overhang. The shakes on its roof were curled and moss-infested, its rough-wood exterior siding darkly weathered. Sitting alone high on the wooded slope, the home reminded Seth of so-called vacation hideaways he'd seen pictures of in magazines.

"Uh-oh," Collin said.

"What?"

Collin darted ahead. At the verge of the driveway, he crouched behind a lilac bush.

Seth, confused, followed.

"That's not good," Collin said.

It took Seth a moment to spy the source of Collin's concern. A band of wide yellow tape encircled the house. Printed repeatedly along the tape, like a shouted warning, were the words SHERIFF'S LINE DO NOT CROSS.

Seth bit his lip. "Why would the police have done that?"

"That's what they do with crime scenes," Collin said.

"Who says it's a crime scene? The deputy said they didn't yet know how Mr. Garber died."

"They must suspect something bad happened to him. Otherwise, why cordon off the house?"

Seth didn't know, and it troubled him. Did the authorities know more about Mr. Garber's death than they were telling? Were his mother's fears valid? Could there be a killer on the loose in the area?

"So, what now?" Collin asked.

Seth brooded over the question. They had climbed this hill for one reason only, and the sheriff's tape didn't change that. "We find the dog."

They crossed the driveway and approached the house. "Here, pooch," Collin called out.

Seth whistled as best he could, but it sounded more like someone trying to imitate gusting wind.

Collin clapped his hands. "Here, doggy."

No dog appeared.

"He's got to be around here somewhere," Seth said. It only made sense that the dog would have returned home. He walked over to the pickup truck, which looked as if it had been parked there for some time. It was heavily coated with dust; pine needles adorned its top and hood; its back window was ripe for a finger-written "wash me" message. He peered under the truck. No dog there.

They checked the garage. Its big retractable door was closed all the way to the ground. A walk-in door on the side was closed and locked as well, and there wasn't a doggy door in it. No way could the dog have gotten inside.

Collin kicked at the gravel in the driveway. "What next?"

"We keep looking," Seth said, not ready to give up.

The boys continued whistling and calling out as they made their way around the house, taking care to stay behind the ribbon of yellow tape. On the west side of the house, they came upon a huge stack of firewood.

"Wow," Collin said, "that's a lot of wood. And look how it's stacked." The firewood was stacked in the round so that it formed a fortress-like cylindrical tower taller than they were. "Never seen anybody stack wood like that around here."

Neither had Seth. "Maybe Mr. Garber wasn't from around here."

The boys moved on, completing the loop around the house without seeing any sign of Garber's dog.

"I don't understand," Seth said. "The dog should be here. This was his home."

Collin picked up a pinecone. "He's probably still down at the pond, waiting for the old man. Dogs do that, you know, when they're abandoned—wait for days, weeks even, for their owners to come back." He flung the pinecone down the driveway. "Why do you care so much anyway? It's only a dog—and a mangy one at that."

"I don't know," Seth said. "I just do."

He knew why he cared so much about the dog. But he also knew that his friend wouldn't under-stand. Collin had never had a dog of his own. That was because his dad raised rabbits. "Dogs and rab-bits don't mix," Collin had told him once. Seth knew that he was merely echoing his father's words.

Years before, when Collin was a toddler, his older brother, Charley, had a dog—a pit bull. He'd gotten it from a school friend in town who'd had to give it up because a neighbor claimed that the dog had killed his cat. "You can keep the dog," Mr. Feeney told Charley, "as long as you keep it away from the rabbits." That wasn't going to be a problem, Charley figured, because all the rabbits were kept in raised, wire-enclosed hutches.

But one day the dog, in a frenzy to get to Mr. Feeney's rabbits, knocked over one of the hutches, causing its door to pop open. The dog mauled to death all the rabbits inside—a mother and twelve babies. When Mr. Feeney found out about it, he shot the dog in the head with a shotgun. He hung its carcass on a fence post and wouldn't let Charley bury it until Mrs. Feeney made such a stink about the stink that he finally relented. When Charley turned sixteen, he ran away from home and never came back. The Feeneys never had a dog after that, and Collin never asked for one.

But, for a time, Seth did have a dog. Rouser, a yellow Lab mix, was six months old when Seth received him for his fifth birthday. He named him Rouser because that's what the dog did. Nights, Rouser slept on a doggy bed on the floor beside Seth's bed. But every morning when daylight came, there was Rouser on top of him, licking his face until he woke up.

A wave of sadness washed over Seth now as he thought about Rouser. When Seth was eight years old, Rouser fell ill. He'd been lethargic for days and ate very little. What he did eat, he threw up. They took him to a pet clinic. It turned out that he was suffering from kidney failure. The veterinarian said it was likely caused by tainted dog food. There'd been a recall of the brand they'd been feeding Rouser.

They took the dog home, and Seth's mother prepared special food for him. He showed signs of improvement. But then he got worse. He stopped eating altogether. He became unsteady on his feet.

His breathing became labored. He started having tremors. He never whined or whimpered, but it was obvious from the way he shied away from being touched that he was in pain. One day, blood appeared in his urine.

Seth's dad took him aside. "Son, I know you don't want to hear this, but I'm afraid the best thing we can do for Rouser now is to have him put to sleep."

"We can't kill him," Seth had cried. But he knew it wasn't fair to Rouser to let him live in pain, so he agreed.

He insisted on going with his dad to the pet clinic to have Rouser put down. He sat on the cold tile floor, cuddling the dog as the vet gave him a shot. Rouser gazed up at him with a confused look. Seth stroked his head. "It's okay, boy." Then Rouser went limp in his arms. It happened so fast.

Seth broke down. He cried on the way home from the vet's office and all that night as well. To be holding a living thing, its heart beating rhythmically, joyously in concert with your own, and then suddenly to feel the life go out of it forever was the most awful feeling imaginable. But he didn't want to talk about it, not then and not now.

"Check that out," Collin said, pointing at the house. "The front door isn't shut all the way."

Seth glanced over, skeptical. But when they moved closer, he saw that the door was indeed cracked open. "It probably just didn't latch fully when the cops closed it, and then the wind blew it open or something."

Collin edged up against the yellow tape barrier. "Maybe the dog went inside." He glanced back at

Seth with that telling gleam in his eyes. "We should go in and find out."

Seth took a step backward. "No way. That's asking for trouble."

"Hey," Collin said, "you're the one all worried about the dog." He ducked under the ribbon of tape and pushed the door open.

"Collin, don't . . ."

His friend disappeared inside the house.

It was just like Collin. Finding the dog had suddenly become a challenge, and Collin always responded to challenges, especially ones that involved taking risks.

Seth stood there staring at the sheriff's tape, its repeated warning blinking in his head like a flashing red light. He stayed put.

Collin stuck his head out the doorway. "You should see this."

"See what?"

Collin retreated inside the house.

Seth groaned. He closed his eyes and counted to ten, hoping the urge to follow his friend went away. It didn't. *I shouldn't be doing this*, he thought as he slipped under the tape and entered the house.

He found Collin in the living room, staring down at a jumble of items on the floor. Envelopes, loose papers, pens and pencils, scissors, a razor knife, a measuring tape, a magnifying glass, a small sewing kit, coins of various denominations, rubber bands, Scotch tape, a glue stick and more lay scattered in front of a small antique-looking wooden desk. The desk's only drawer—empty—stood on end against one leg of the desk.

Seth frowned. "What a mess. Who would have done this?"

"The sheriff's deputies were here," Collin said. "But *they* wouldn't have done this." He poked at some of the items with his foot. "You know what I think—I think someone else was here, and they were looking for something."

"But who? And what?"

"I don't know. Let's check out the rest of the house."

"We should go," Seth said.

"Just a quick look around first," Collin said and headed down a hallway to the back of the house.

Seth glanced around nervously. "Okay, but really quick."

It didn't take long to go through the house. Besides a small living room, it had a combination kitchen-dining area, one bathroom, and two bedrooms. It was sparsely furnished, and what furniture it had was, as Seth's dad would have put it, *broken in and then some.*

And there was something strange about one of the bedrooms. While the first one they came to had a bed and dresser, the second one was empty except for a sleeping bag laid out on the bare hardwood floor. And the oddest thing—all the panes of glass in the room's only window had been painted black. It didn't make any sense.

"I don't know what somebody could have been looking for," Seth said as the boys returned to the living room. "It's hard to imagine that Mr. Garber kept anything of value here. This place is pretty shabby."

Collin shrugged. "He could have hid money in the house, and somebody found out about it. Some old people do that. They don't trust banks, so they stash bills in socks and books and cookie jars and places like that."

"He didn't live like he had money to hide."

"Maybe he had guns," Collin said. "People break into homes all the time to steal guns."

The mention of guns gave Seth a start. "We'd better get out of here. We don't want to get blamed for stealing guns—or anything."

But Collin had stopped listening. Something in the far corner of the room, next to a wood-burning stove, had caught his attention. He went over to a rack of fireplace tools and seized the handle of a long, bladed object. "Wicked," he said, pulling it from the rack. "Garber stirred his ashes with a bayonet."

Seth drew back at the sight of the thing. He had no qualms about attacking berry vines with a machete. But the grooved blade of a bayonet was made for one thing—killing. "Put it back," he said, "and let's get out of here."

Collin thrust the bayonet at an imaginary enemy. "The deputy said Mr. Garber was a veteran, right? He must have fought in a war." He grazed a finger along the length of the blade. "You think he killed someone with this?"

"Collin, put it—"

The sound of a dog barking silenced him. The barking came from behind the house. No—now from out front—sharp, repetitive barking. It was the kind of fuss Rouser had made whenever a stranger appeared on their property unexpectedly. But what was this yelping all about?

The boys rushed to the living room window and looked out just in time to see a man running away from the house, down the driveway. A dog—Mr. Garber's dog—stood in the driveway barking at the man.

Seth gasped. "Who's that? And where did he come from?"

Collin's gaze flitted around the room. "I bet it's the person who made this mess." His eyes grew big. "He was probably in the house when we came in."

Seth shivered at the thought. "We need to get out of here before that guy—or someone else—comes back." This little adventure had definitely not gone as planned.

Collin hastily reracked the bayonet.

When the boys bolted from the house, Garber's dog was still in the driveway barking at the man, who was now out of sight.

Collin made a beeline for the trees on the downslope.

"Wait!" Seth hollered.

"For what?" Collin said, coming to a sliding stop.

"We have to take the dog."

Collin screwed up his face. "You gotta be kidding."

Seth stood his ground.

"Okay," Collin said, shaking his head. "We take the dog—if we can catch it."

9

"**COME HERE, BOY,**" Seth said in a honeyed voice. As ready as he was to flee, he couldn't bear the thought of leaving the dog behind.

"Good doggy," Collin said, making a kissy-smoochy sound through puckered lips.

The dog kept its distance, facing them with an aggressive stance: stiff body, erect ears, white-eyed stare. It wasn't a big dog, but big enough to be taken seriously. Whenever the boys moved closer, the dog backed away, growling through bared teeth.

"Poor thing," Seth said, not wanting to force the issue. "It's scared." It was also very scruffy-looking. Its shaggy gray hair bristled with dried mud, reminding Seth of a frayed Brillo pad. He tried again to allay the dog's fear. "It's okay, fella. You can trust us. We want to help you."

But no amount of coaxing could persuade the dog to come to them.

"Can we go now?" Collin said.

"Stay here," Seth said. "I'll be right back."

His thoughts of Rouser had given him an idea. He

hurried back inside Garber's house and rummaged through the old man's refrigerator, finding just the thing to bridge the gap between himself and a frightened dog.

Back outside, he knelt down and dangled the wiener out in front of him. The dog's nose twitched, but the pooch held its ground. Seth tore off a chunk of wiener and tossed it onto the ground a few feet in front of the dog. The dog shot forward and gobbled it up.

Seth tore off another portion and lobbed it toward the dog, this time making it move closer to him to get its prize. Again, the dog devoured the meat. Then it stood there eying Seth, looking more expectant now than threatening.

Encouraged, Seth pinched off a third piece of wiener and dropped it a few feet ahead of himself. The dog stayed put, staring at the offering, drool dripping from its muzzle. Seth waited. Finally, warily, the dog inched forward and snatched up the morsel.

Almost there, Seth thought. But now the hardest part. He placed a bit of the meat in his palm. His hand shook as he held it out to the dog. The dog hesitated, its eyes darting around. Then hunger overcoming fear, it came forward and ate from Seth's hand.

While Seth fed the rest of the wiener to the dog, Collin took off his belt and looped it through the dog's collar to fashion a crude leash. "Got him."

Seth patted the dog's head. "Attaboy." The dog stood there with its tongue hanging out, panting. "I think it needs water."

They found a plastic bowl outside the back door of

the house. At an outside faucet, Seth rinsed out the bowl and filled it with water. The dog lapped at it eagerly.

"Now can we get out of here?" Collin said.

With Seth holding the improvised leash, they walked the dog down Mr. Garber's driveway to Fir Hill Road. Now that they'd given it food and water, the dog seemed perfectly willing to go with them.

Fir Hill Road ended at Garber's driveway. The quickest way to Collin's house from there was to continue down the wooded slope and reconnect with the access road at the base of the hillside. From there it was a short walk to Collin's house.

Seth picked the dog up. Hugging it to his chest, he carried it through the underbrush, his forearms shielding it from the backlash of brushed-aside branches. Once they reached the road, he put it down on the ground.

"I don't think my mom's gonna like me bringing a dog home," Collin said.

"Does this dog look like a rabbit killer?" As soon as the words were out of his mouth, Seth was sorry he'd spoken them. "Anyway," he added, wanting to gloss over his insensitive remark, "it's only for a little while, until we figure out what to do with it. We need a plan." Seth's plan, of course, was to convince his parents to let him keep the dog. But he needed time to think about how to accomplish that.

At Collin's house, his mother's car was gone from its usual place in the driveway. Collin went into the house and came back out right away. "She's probably gone shopping," he said, sounding relieved.

Seth sat down on the Feeney's front porch steps

with the dog at his feet. He riffled his fingers through the dog's matted hair. "We need to give this guy a bath."

"How do you know it's a guy?" Collin said. "It's got so much mud clinging to its underbelly, you can't see what kind of thing it has."

Seth hopped up and led the dog down the steps. "A bath it is, then."

Collin unraveled a garden hose attached to a spigot at the front of the house. "You better keep a good grip on the belt," he said, turning the water on. "The dog might not like this."

But the dog stood still as Collin ran water over its haunches and scrubbed its mud-clotted coat. "Definitely a guy," he said after he'd washed off enough muck to expose dangling testicles.

"You have an old towel or something to dry him off with?" Seth asked.

Before Collin could respond, the dog shook vigorously. Water droplets flew in every direction, drenching the boys. "Never mind," Seth said, laughing.

Collin was laughing too. Then he stopped laughing when he saw his mother's SUV pull into the driveway.

She got out of the vehicle and opened its cargo hatch. "Boys, help me with these groceries."

Seth buckled the dog's belt-leash around a spindle on the porch railing, and the boys went to help Collin's mom.

She handed each of them a bulging bag. "Where'd that mutt come from?"

An alarm bell went off in Seth's head. He waited for Collin to answer.

"We found it on our way over here from Seth's house," Collin said.

Seth let out a silent sigh of relief.

Collin's mom tucked her purse under her arm, grabbed a jug of milk, and headed for the front door. "Well, someone better call animal control and have them come pick it up before your father gets home from work."

"Why?" Collin said as the boys followed her into the house.

"You know why."

Seth's heart skipped a beat. "But Mrs. Feeney, it's Mr. Garber's dog. You know, the man . . . from the pond."

"Hmm . . . Is that so?"

"Yes, ma'am."

They carried the groceries into the kitchen.

"Set the bags on the counter," Collin's mother said.

The boys made one more trip to bring in the rest of the groceries before going back outside. Seth unbuckled the belt-leash from the railing, and they sat down on the porch steps with the dog huddled between them, still leashed.

"Mom's right," Collin said. "It wouldn't be good for the dog to be here when my dad gets home."

Seth knew that was so, and he knew why. He just wasn't sure what to do about it. He didn't want to get his friend in trouble, but the thought of turning the dog over to animal control triggered an unpleasant tightness around his heart. "I'll take the dog to my house and figure something out."

"Yeah," Collin said with a sly grin, "he doesn't

look like a chicken killer."

Seth felt his cheeks burning. He ran his hand along the dog's back, smoothing its coat. "No, he doesn't."

"Just make sure you've got lots of wieners on hand."

"Right," Seth said, and the seriousness of the moment dissolved like a breaking fever.

Collin's mom came out of the house then and passed Collin a slip of paper with some numbers written on it.

"What's this?"

"The non-emergency telephone number for the sheriff's department." She handed him a cordless phone. "If this dog really belonged to that dead man, then someone needs to call the sheriff's office and let them know it's been found. You boys found the dog, so it's your responsibility to make the call. Ask for that deputy you talked to at the pond. What was his name?"

Collin shot Seth a troubled look. "I don't remember," he said, almost surely lying.

"Then remember harder," his mother said and went back inside.

"I don't want to call," Collin said, holding the phone away from his body as if it were radioactive.

"Not me," Seth said. "Your house, your phone."

In the end, the boys flipped for it, using a nickel Collin got from his mother. They would have done rock, paper, scissors, but Seth always lost at that game. He figured his chances of winning a coin toss were better. He was wrong.

Collin pocketed the coin. "Should have asked for a quarter."

Seth sat staring at the phone in his hand, trying to think of a way out of making the call. Was it too late for him to take the dog and go home? If he did leave with the dog, then what? He thought and thought but couldn't conjure up a *then what* that wouldn't lead them deeper into the quagmire of half-truths he'd already gotten himself and his friend into.

His finger twitched as he punched in the number. When a voice answered, he asked to speak with Deputy Waller, hoping with all his might that the deputy was not available. His luck wasn't any better this time.

"What can I do for you, Seth?" Waller asked.

Seth told him about finding Mr. Garber's dog. When the deputy asked where they'd found it, Seth parroted the response Collin had given his mother.

"Very well," Waller said. "You boys stay put with the dog. I have one other call to follow up on, and then I'll come out and check out the area around where you found the poor fellow. I don't know what we can learn, but it's worth a look-see."

Seth told Collin what the deputy had said.

"We're dead meat," Collin said.

"Maggot pie," Seth said.

"Pond scum."

"Compost."

"Dog vomit."

Seth's shoulders sagged. His bright hopes for the day were gone, replaced by a darkening gloom.

"Although . . ." Collin said, the lilt in his voice inviting wishful thinking.

"Although what?" Seth asked. Was there a way out of this mess he hadn't thought of?

Collin hedged. "There might be a way to save our skin, but you won't like it."

Seth stared at his friend, guardedly hopeful. "Tell me anyway."

"We let the dog go."

Seth recoiled. "Let him go?" That would never have crossed his mind. It was contrary to the whole purpose of finding the dog—his purpose anyway.

"Yeah," Collin said. "If we let the dog go—say that he got loose and ran away—then maybe the deputy wouldn't care where we found him. Then we'd be off the hook."

"I don't know," Seth said, shaking his head. The very suggestion depressed him.

"You got a better idea?"

Seth didn't.

"Okay, then," Collin said, "I say we do it."

"But . . ." Seth gritted his teeth and held his peace.

Collin slid the belt free of the dog's collar. He flapped his hands. "Go on, boy. Go home."

The dog didn't budge.

"Shoo," Collin said, giving the dog a nudge.

The dog put his front paws on Seth's lap.

Seth ruffled the dog's ears. "I don't think he wants to go anywhere."

"Yep," Collin said, looking woeful. "Dead meat—that's what we are."

Seth sat quietly, thinking. "I should call my mom," he finally said. "It'll be better if I tell her over the phone."

"Tell her what?" Collin's mom said. She was standing behind them in the doorway.

"Oh boy," Collin muttered.

Seth exhaled heavily, resigning himself to his fate; it was going to come out sooner or later anyway. "Where we really found the dog."

10

THE DAY WAS WARMING. The morning breeze had died away. A few thin clouds, like wisps of smoke, drifted across an otherwise clear blue sky. Slanting sunlight crept up the porch steps, where the boys sat in a mindless funk awaiting Deputy Waller's arrival.

After giving up on the idea of letting Mr. Garber's dog go, the boys had retied him to the porch railing with some old clothesline rope, allowing enough line for him to retreat into the shade under the porch, where they'd placed a pan of water. "Drink up, boy," Seth said, sloshing his fingers in the pan. The dog lapped up some water and then trotted along behind the boys as they returned to the steps.

"You'd probably be better off staying under the porch, boy," Seth said as he petted the dog.

"We'd probably *all* be better off under the porch," Collin said with a joyless chuckle.

Before the deputy arrived at Collin's house, Seth's mother appeared. Leaving her minivan parked askew in the driveway, she stomped up the porch steps. "Inside," she ordered the boys and entered the house without knocking. Garber's dog slunk out of sight under the porch.

The two moms took turns yelling at the boys. "That man could have killed you both!" Seth's mom cried, her face red with indignation. "All because of some stupid dog!" Collin's mother took over from there with no less fury in her voice.

The boys were actually relieved when Deputy Waller got there. The deputy, while displeased upon hearing the full story of how and where they found the dog, lectured the boys calmly—though no less soberly. "This is serious," he said, fixing his gaze on them where they sat flanked by their ill-humored mothers on the Feeneys' sectional sofa. "Trespassing—going onto someone else's property without permission—is a crime. To make matters worse, you crossed a barrier put there by the sheriff's department expressly to keep people out."

The words fell heavily on Seth's ears and he felt the sting of his remorse for what he and Collin had done. But what pained him most was the look of disappointment on his mother's face. He wished that he could say something to make it go away. But what was there to say other than he was sorry? He'd already said that several times, so he stayed mum, fighting back tears.

"We just wanted to find the dog," Collin said.

"And that's commendable," the deputy said. "But you shouldn't have broken the law to do it."

"Are we going to jail?" Collin asked.

For his part, Seth was less concerned about going to jail than he was about going home with his mother.

"Now let's not get ahead of ourselves," Waller said. "At this point, I just want to make sure I have all the facts. So let's talk more about this man you saw at Garber's house. Was it someone you'd seen before?"

"We didn't get a good look at him," Collin said.

"We only saw him from behind as he ran away," Seth added.

The deputy took out his pen and notepad. "Okay, let's see what we can learn from that. Was he tall or short?"

"He wasn't tall, but he wasn't short either," Collin said.

Seth nodded in agreement.

"What about his build? Was he slim or stocky?"

The boys exchanged looks of uncertainty.

"He was . . . in between," Seth said.

"All right," the deputy said and kept asking these either-or questions until he was satisfied the boys had told him everything they knew. He took a few moments to review his notes. "Here's what we've got then: Our mystery man is an adult male of medium height and build, with short dark hair and light skin, wearing gray slacks and a white short-sleeved shirt with a collar. Is that about right?"

The boys said it was.

The deputy put away his notepad. "Here's what I'd like to do," he said, addressing the two moms. "With your permission, I'd like to take the boys back up to Garber's place, where I'll have them walk me through everything they saw and did while they were there. I'll send an officer ahead to secure the scene. After we're done, I'll bring the boys back here and we'll have another talk. You can accompany us if you'd like, but you don't have to."

The moms gave their consent. Both declined to go along.

"You tell the deputy everything," Seth's mother instructed the boys as they climbed into the backseat of the cruiser. "And I mean *everything*."

And the boys did.

11

WHEN DEPUTY WALLER brought the boys back to Collin's house, their dads were there also. The deputy pulled his cruiser in behind Mr. Feeney's pickup.

"Whoa," Collin said in a croaky voice. "I'm in for it now."

Seth, on the other hand, was pleased to see his dad's Taurus parked off to the side. Not that his dad's presence meant he was in any less trouble. It was just that his dad tended to take bad news more calmly than his mom did. "There are always two sides to every issue," his dad would say, while his mom viewed an issue from only one side—hers.

"After you, boys," the deputy said, directing them up the front steps.

Seth lingered long enough to glance under the porch. He was relieved to see Mr. Garber's dog lying there, blanketed by shadow. The dog looked up at him but made no move to come out. *Poor fellow is still scared*, Seth thought. With all this commotion, it was no wonder. But at least Mr. Feeney hadn't shot him.

Inside the house, tension filled the living room like a suffocating heat, a lot of it coming from Collin's dad. Still dressed in his work clothes—sap-stained denim jeans supported by suspenders, scuffed leather boots, and a sawdust-dappled T-shirt—he stood in the kitchen doorway with his arms folded across his chest and a scowl on his face.

The other parents, striking their own rigid poses, sat on the sofa. Whatever conversation might have been taking place ceased the moment the boys, followed by Deputy Waller, entered the room.

Seth's dad stood and shook hands with the deputy. Collin's dad stayed put.

"Have a seat," Collin's mom said to Waller, indicating an armchair. She pointed at two straight-backed chairs off to the side. "Boys—join us."

Seth had never been in a courtroom, but he had the sinking feeling that an unofficial trial had taken place here during his and Collin's absence. Now a judgment was about to be rendered in the case of Parents versus Wayward Sons—and not by a sympathetic jury.

"Thank you all for being here," the deputy said as he and the boys seated themselves. "It saves me from having to speak with each family separately. First, let me say that the boys and I have come to an understanding. They'll stay away from Mr. Garber's house and, for now, they won't face any charges. Nevertheless, I'll have to file a report, and there could still be consequences."

"There'll be consequences all right," Mr. Feeney muttered, and Seth feared for his friend's welfare. He'd seen the welts on Collin's backside after one of his whippings.

A moment of awkward silence followed before Collin's mom, addressing the deputy, spoke up. "What kind of consequences?"

"Well, the boys *were* trespassing," Waller said. "And they crossed a police line. I could cite them for hindering an investigation, but considering their age and lack of criminal intent, I don't think that's called for. The boys have promised that, from now on, they'll leave the investigating up to the police. Right, boys?"

The boys nodded, then they looked at their parents and nodded some more.

"What about the man the boys saw running away?" Seth's mother asked, anxiety flashing in her eyes like dancing waters. "What do you think he was doing there? And what if he comes back?"

"I believe he was looking for something," the deputy said, "but I'm not sure what."

"Money, drugs, guns," Mr. Feeney said. "Some meth-head, no doubt."

"Maybe," Waller said. "But it appears that he may have simply been looking for information."

"Information?" said Mrs. Feeney, her heavily penciled eyebrows knitting.

"Yes, what you can learn about a person from the things you might expect to find in a desk—bills, address books, photos, calendars, and the like. I'm not certain that's what he was looking for, but if it was, then he would have been sorely disappointed. I know that because our people had already searched the house and uncovered surprisingly little personal information about Henry Garber. The man obviously wasn't into recordkeeping or accumulating memorabilia."

"But why would someone be looking for information about Mr. Garber?" Seth's mother asked.

Seth wondered that also.

"I don't know," Waller said. "But I don't think whoever it was will be back. Either he found what he was looking for or he didn't. We have the boys' description of the man, and I'll have an evidence tech check the house for fingerprints and DNA evidence. If we're lucky, he'll come up with something we can follow up on. But I don't think you have to worry about the man returning. As a precaution, I'll have a deputy do an occasional drive-by. And if any of you see anyone suspicious hanging around in the area, call the sheriff's department and we'll send a unit out right away. Any more questions?"

Seth was afraid to speak up, but he couldn't hold back. "What about the dog?" he asked, keeping his eyes downcast.

"The dog . . . right," Waller said, as if that had slipped his mind. "I'll have the animal control officer pick him up and take him to the animal shelter. They'll find him a good home."

Seth's head jerked up. "But—"

A sharp look from his mother cut him off. "Don't even think about it," she said.

Seth's dad, who had yet to say anything, addressed the deputy. "Any word from the VA on Mr. Garber's next of kin? It would help if someone took possession of his property."

The deputy shook his head. "I'm afraid we still

don't have any leads in that regard. The VA's records show that Mr. Garber received services at the Roseburg VA hospital as an outpatient. But he never designated a next of kin or gave an emergency contact number. It appears that he didn't have any family in the area, or if he did, he'd cut all ties with them."

No family? An image arose in Seth's mind of the medical examiner zipping closed the black bag containing Mr. Garber's body. Sadness welled up inside him, filling his chest. A disturbing thought followed, and again he was unable to stay silent. "So if no next of kin is found, what happens to Mr. Garber? I mean to his . . . you know. . ."

"His remains?" the deputy said.

Seth nodded.

"That's none of your concern," his mother said.

"Actually, that's a fair question," Deputy Waller said, "and it deserves an answer. Because the sad reality is that dead bodies go unclaimed all too often. Some of the unclaimed are homeless. Some are estranged from family. Some—like Mr. Garber—are veterans. And it's not just a local problem. It's a national tragedy."

His aspect darkened with the seriousness of his words. "We don't know if that will happen in this case; we hope not. So all I can tell you for sure is this: After the medical examiner is through with Mr. Garber's body, it will be sent to a local mortuary and held for final disposition. Oregon law states that if no one claims a body within ten days, the mortuary is free to dispose of it by turning it over to an approved research institution or by cremating or burying it in the least costly manner."

He flashed his palms as if to say, *it's out of my hands.* "So if no one steps forward to claim Henry Garber's body, that's what will happen."

But that's not what 'should' happen! Seth wanted to say. *Not to Mr. Garber—not to anyone!* But he felt the power of his mother's gaze, and he kept the words to himself.

12

IT WAS QUIET around the Robersons' dinner table that night. Even chatterbox Baylie was subdued. Seth thought she must be sick or something, because otherwise she'd be jabbering away faster than anyone could listen even if they wanted to.

He took an occasional bite of food but mostly just rearranged it on his plate as if playing a game of musical chairs with it. He knew that he was facing some punishment, a sentence to be handed down by his dad. It was always his dad who issued the discipline. That struck Seth as odd, since it was his mother who seemed devoted to the parenting principle that *no misbehavior should go unpunished.*

One time he got in trouble at school for shooting spitballs through a straw at other students in the lunchroom. It didn't matter that he hadn't started the spitball fight; it only mattered that he was the one who got caught. While lying in bed that night, he overheard his parents discussing his punishment.

"He won't learn anything, David, if you keep coddling him," his mother said.

"I don't coddle him," his father responded. "I just don't think we need to burn him at the stake to show him the error of his ways."

His sentence that time was no TV or video games for a month. But now he was facing judgment for a far more serious offense.

He took a bite of food, swallowed it without enjoyment, and set his fork down on his plate. "Can I go to my room now?"

Seth's dad shot a look at his mom. She avoided his gaze.

"Go ahead," his dad told him. "I'll be up later to talk to you." And Seth knew what that meant.

In his room, he slumped onto the floor alongside his bed and pondered his impending punishment. What had Collin said? *I'm in for it now.* Well, *he* was in for it too—not a whipping like Collin would get, but something more severe than a ban on TV time and video games. Yet, in a way, he wasn't sorry for the trouble he was in, because otherwise they wouldn't have found Mr. Garber's dog.

Thinking about the dog brought back to mind the image of Mr. Garber's body laid out on the bank of the pond. It still disturbed him to think of what would happen if no one came forward to claim it. His mother had said it was none of his concern. *But it should be someone's concern! If not mine, then whose?*

There was a knock on his bedroom door. The door opened and his dad came into the room. He sat down on the bed and had Seth sit beside him.

"First of all, son," he said, "I want you to know that I'm not angry with you. Disappointed, yes."

"Mom's angry."

"Yes, she is. But that's only because she doesn't want anything bad to happen to you."

"Like what happened to Mr. Garber."

"Well . . . yes. We don't know how he died, but we know that there was an intruder in his house. So your mom is worried about your safety. Can you understand that?"

"Yessir."

"And do you understand that what you and Collin did today was wrong?"

"It was stupid," Seth said. "And for sure I'll never do anything like that again."

His dad smiled. "In that case, we're halfway there."

Seth knew what the other half was—his punishment. But something else occupied his thoughts at the moment. "Dad?"

"Yes?"

"It isn't right, you know."

"What isn't right?"

"That Mr. Garber's body should go unclaimed. And if it does, then the mortuary can do whatever it wants with it. It's just not right. Mr. Garber was alone in life, and that's bad enough. But now it's like he's alone in death too. His house is vacant with no one to look after it, and his dog has to go to the animal shelter. And it probably won't get adopted because, like Collin says, it's scraggly."

His dad sighed. "No, son, it isn't right. And it's very caring of you to feel that way. But tell me, why all this concern for someone you didn't know?"

"I don't know," Seth said. "It's just . . . it's just . . ." But he didn't have a good answer.

"Is it because you and Collin found the body, and now you feel a sense of obligation toward the man?"

"Maybe." But Seth knew there was more to it than that. The sentiment came from deep inside him—from a place of knowing without understanding. "Dad, don't you just sometimes feel a certain way about something and you don't know why?"

"I guess so."

"Well, that's the way I feel about this. There's got to be someone out there willing to claim Mr. Garber's body—a friend or family member. Can't we do something to help find them?"

His dad shook his head. "As unfortunate as the situation is, it's probably not a good idea for us to become involved. Besides, I don't know what we can do that the police haven't already done."

Seth thought he knew. "Deputy Waller said that Mr. Garber had been a patient at the local VA hospital. Don't you have a friend who works there? You could talk to him. Maybe he can help. Maybe he knew Mr. Garber, or knows someone who did."

"I don't know. Like I said—"

"But you could at least talk to him, Dad, couldn't you?"

"I . . . uh." Moments passed in silence. His dad cleared his throat. He nodded. "Sure, son, I can do that."

"Thanks, Dad," Seth said, still not sure why it mattered so much to him, but grateful nonetheless. "And Dad, I really have learned my lesson about interfering in police business."

"Good."

"But I know I still have to be punished."

"Yes, you do," his dad said. He clasped Seth's shoulder and gave it a gentle squeeze. "But we'll save that for tomorrow."

"Right," Seth said. "Tomorrow."

Now he had all night to worry about what his punishment would be.

13

AS IT TURNED OUT, it was Seth's *mother* who imposed his punishment, although she insisted it wasn't punishment at all.

Seth was of a different opinion. "I don't want to go stay with Grandma Claire," he protested. The very idea of it gave him a stomachache. "Her apartment is tiny, and there's nothing to do in town. Anyway, I thought she was in Minnesota."

"She got back yesterday. I talked to her last evening, and she'll be here any time now to pick you up."

"But Mom . . ."

"No buts," she said in her and-that's-final voice. "Your dad and I agreed."

Seth clenched his fists in frustration. "Why don't you just whip me? That's what Collin's parents do."

His mother gave him a hard stare. "We are *not* Collin's parents." She held the stare long enough to wilt his defiance. "Now, as soon as you're done with your breakfast, get your travel bag and pack some clothes—enough for a week. If you need more, I'll bring them later. And don't forget underwear and socks."

Seth pushed his half-eaten bowl of Cheerios aside. Suddenly, he wasn't the least bit hungry. His dad had already left for work. Baylie was bouncing around the house, all excited about going to Brownie Camp. Guess she wasn't sick after all. He'd been trying to enjoy his last meal before sentencing was pronounced. He couldn't believe that his parents were really going to banish him to his grandmother's apartment in town—for a week or more!

His mother cleared his cereal bowl from the table. "If you're not going to eat any more, then go on and get to packing. And don't be so glum about it. You should be happy to be spending time with your grandmother."

He wasn't.

In his room, he pulled his canvas travel bag out of the closet and tossed it onto the bed. Then he tossed himself onto the bed. This was the worst punishment ever. Worse than losing TV and video game time, or being given extra chores, or having to go to bed early, or . . . anything else he could think of. What a way to ruin a perfectly good summer vacation!

He loved his grandmother. She was nice to him, and he could talk her into things he couldn't talk his parents into, like going to see PG-13 movies and letting him eat all the ice cream he wanted. He enjoyed the occasional brief visits with her. But the thought of staying with her in her apartment for days on end was depressing.

The apartment was nice enough. It was in a good part of town, and Grandma Claire had nice things.

That wasn't the problem. The problem was that *it was an apartment! In town!* There were neighbors on the other side of the walls. Outside her front door was a parking lot. Outside her back door was a fenced-in patio the size of a chicken run, and beyond that were *more apartments!*

Seth had liked it better when his grandmother lived in the house just down the road from them. He and Collin could pop in for a visit anytime, get a hug and a home-baked treat, and be on their merry way. But that place was too much for her to take care of, she'd said. On top of that, most of her friends lived in town now—the ones she played pinochle with on Tuesdays and quilted with on Thursdays and met at the Y twice a week for chair yoga. "Country living is for young people," she had said in announcing her decision to move to town, "and I'm not young anymore."

But Seth *was* young, and he loved living in the country. Until he was old enough to go to school and visit the homes of some of his classmates—for birthday parties mostly—he hadn't even realized there was a way of life other than his own.

In town, houses butted up against each other like nests in a henhouse, their backyards no bigger than his mother's bean patch. Rules prohibited shooting guns and keeping barnyard animals. You couldn't ride a bike on the streets without being a target for hurried drivers. And the nerve-jarring sounds: wailing sirens and honking horns were the birdcalls of the city. Even though his home was only five miles out of town, it could have been on another planet for all the difference it made in how he lived.

"Seth, your grandmother is here." His mother's call resounded up the stairwell like the voice of doom.

He grabbed his travel bag and crammed it with clothes from his chest of drawers.

"I'M GLAD YOU'LL BE SPENDING some time with me," Grandma Claire said in her naturally husky voice. "I could use your help."

They were approaching the Roseburg city limits. His grandmother was speeding as usual. "She drives like a teenager," Seth's dad had once commented. "She'll end up overturned in a ditch someday." Seth hoped it wasn't today.

"My help with what?" he asked.

"Ladder work."

"What kind of ladder work?"

"The kind my old legs aren't good for anymore."

At his grandmother's apartment, Seth hauled his travel bag into the spare bedroom. He'd been in the room before but had never slept there. Anytime his parents were gone from home overnight, Grandma Claire came to their house to stay with him and Baylie. Sometimes Baylie spent a weekend in town with her. But she was a girl, and girls were easily occupied with city stuff like shopping and tea parties.

His grandmother poked her head into the room. "I want to take the quilt off that bed and put on a lighter spread. Why don't we do that now."

"Okay," Seth said, trying his best to mask his disappointment at being there. After all, it wasn't her fault his parents had come up with such drastic punishment for his misdeeds. "Did you make this one?" he asked as they lifted the quilt off the bed.

"It's pretty." He liked it because its panels depicted birds in various settings: birds perched on branches, birds in flight, birds in nests with tiny eggs.

"Yes, I made it. Our quilting group makes quilts for a local homeless shelter. But I just couldn't give this one up."

He helped her fold it. "It must have taken a long time to make."

"Yes, our club is the only one I know of in town that still stitches by hand."

His grandmother stored the quilt on a shelf in the closet. They covered the bed with a lightweight spread, pale blue with embroidered pink and white flower petals. "Better for summer sleeping," she said. She rubbed her hands together gleefully. "Now how about we play some gin rummy?"

Seth shrugged. "I guess." What else was there to do?

They played at the kitchen table. The table was covered with a red-and-black checkered tablecloth, which made Seth think they should have been playing checkers. His chances of winning might have been better; Grandma Claire was a very good card player. Old and wrinkled as she was, she still had a quick mind. When they had played three hands, she was already eighty points ahead.

She shuffled the cards and dealt another hand, doing it with surprising dexterity, Seth thought, considering those knobby-knuckled fingers of hers.

"I hope you're not letting me win because I'm an old lady and you feel sorry for me."

Seth picked up his cards and began arranging them in his hand. "I'm just giving you a head start."

In truth, he was distracted by thoughts of what had brought him there. He took the upcard, added it to his hand, and discarded. "Did Mom tell you what Collin and I did to get in trouble?"

His grandmother pounced on his discard. "She did." She frowned. "Not the smartest thing you've ever done."

Seth felt himself getting smaller in his chair. "I know."

His grandmother discarded. "She also told me about you boys finding that poor man's body in the pond. That must have been awful."

Seth passed on her discard. "You never liked him, did you?" He drew a card from the stock.

"Liked who?"

"Mr. Garber."

Grandma Claire's brow tweaked. "What makes you say that?"

Seth stared at the arrangement of cards in his hand. "You always said we should keep our distance from him."

"That's only because he was . . . different."

"You mean, because he was a loner?"

"Among other things."

"What other things?"

Her expression clouded. "I don't know. Just a feeling I got."

"Did he do anything to give you that feeling? Like harass you or something?"

"Goodness no," his grandmother said. "I hardly ever saw him, and only from a distance when he was down at the pond." She waved a hand in front of her as if to clear the air of smoke. "Now let's concentrate on the game. You have a lot of catching up to do."

But Seth wanted to finish the conversation. "How long did he live in that house on the hill?"

Grandma Claire let out an audible breath. She laid her cards facedown on the table and sat back in her chair. She brushed back some wayward strands of her silvery gray hair. "He moved up there several years after your grandfather and I bought our place there in the valley."

"Then you've known him a long time?"

"I've known . . . that he lived in the neighborhood."

"Did you ever talk to him?" Seth asked.

"Once," his grandmother said, "when he first moved there. But that was way before you were born." She picked up her cards. "Now play. You're stalling."

"Do you know anything about his family?"

Her jaw muscles twitched as she stared at her cards. "Why would I?"

Seth shrugged. "The deputy said he was a veteran. Collin and I saw his bayonet."

"Bayonet?"

"We think he used it as a poker for his wood-stove."

Grandma Claire's eyelids fluttered. "I told you he was different."

"Is being different a bad thing?"

She pursed her lips. "No, I guess not."

"Gin," Seth said and laid down his combinations.

"Oh, you sneaky little boy."

14

FOR SETH, AS FOR MOST BOYS, summertime was a happy, carefree time of year. That's because it meant *no school*, and *no school* equaled freedom. Freedom from his mother's alarm-clock voice breaching his cocoon of sleep, freedom from the tiresome bus ride to and from school, freedom from the constraints of the classroom, freedom from homework! A brilliant summer's morning was a harbinger of adventures to come. A balmy summer's evening was a trumpet call to milk every drop of joy from what remained of the day.

But as he awoke that morning in his grandmother's apartment, Seth felt none of the elation that, like a sugar rush, usually accompanied the dawning of a summer day. In its place, he felt the drumbeat of despair. His vacation was being sabotaged. Moment by moment, day by day, it was slipping away from him, as if pages were being torn from his life's calendar. And he could do nothing about it.

He got out of bed and drew open the curtains of the only window in the room. Indirect sunlight brightened the room, but not his mood. His view was of a run of weathered wooden fencing and, a few feet beyond that, the drab brown siding of another apartment building, a clone of the one he'd inhabited for the last four days.

He slid the window open, sniffed the air, and promptly shut it. The previous day men had come to the apartment complex with noisy machinery and truckloads of asphalt. They'd repaved the parking lot. When they were done, they hauled off their equipment. But as a memorial to their handiwork, they left behind the lingering stench of freshly laid asphalt.

He pulled his trousers on, sat down on the edge of the bed, and sighed. He was dying of boredom. His grandmother was thoroughly content to spend her days watching television (*Enough of cooking shows, already!*), knitting afghans (*Would he like to learn? No.*), or running to the store to pick up whatever it was she'd forgotten to buy the last time she'd run to the store (*Did he care to go along? Yes, anything to get out of the apartment!*).

If she wasn't doing any of those things, she was talking to someone—on the phone, across the fence, over a cup of tea at the kitchen table. Talk, talk, talk. And about what? Nothing Seth cared about. And all the while, summer was wasting away like ripe fruit left on the vine. It was agonizing.

Last evening, he'd called Collin and was bummed to find out that, after getting a whipping from his dad (one that really hurt), he wasn't restricted in any way. And here Seth was doing prison time!

"Not much fun though without you here," Collin said. "When you coming home?"

"I wish I knew," Seth told him.

He put on his socks and shoes and sat staring at a painting of a zebra hanging on the wall. It wasn't like any zebra he'd ever seen. He'd been to Wildlife Safari, the drive-through wildlife sanctuary in Winston, several times with his family. He'd seen real-life zebras there. They had black and white stripes. But the stripes on this zebra were every color of the rainbow. It was unnatural, like . . . *like being caged inside an apartment!*

Grandma Claire had told him that he could go outside and play as long as he stayed within the apartment complex. But there was nothing for him to do out there. There was an open area with picnic tables and barbecue grills, but no play equipment for kids.

"Why isn't there a playground here?" he asked his grandmother.

"What for? This is a seniors-only community. You have to be at least fifty-five years old to live here."

"Then what am I doing here?"

His grandmother smiled thinly. "I think you know that as well as I do."

After the first couple of days at the apartment, Seth had thought things couldn't get any worse. Then came quilting night and his grandmother insisted he go with her. It was held in a big room at the local seniors' center. A bunch of old ladies wielding needles and thread sat around tables sewing mismatched pieces of cloth together as if they didn't know you could buy a quilt at Walmart for twenty dollars.

And, of course, his grandmother had to introduce him to everyone. "This is my grandson," she said, loud enough to shake the walls. "He's staying with me for a few days. He thinks it's punishment, but someday he'll feel differently."

The old ladies stomped their feet. One of them offered to give him a lesson in hand stitching. He said he'd rather watch. He watched until he couldn't keep his eyes open any longer. His grandmother woke him when it was time to leave. On their way home, he asked her why the women had stomped their feet when she'd introduced him. "It's their way of clapping so as not to stab themselves with their needles," she said.

Seth got up and walked across the hall to the bathroom. He relieved himself, washed his hands, and splashed water on his face. When he entered the kitchen, he found his grandmother standing at the sink rinsing out a plastic bucket. Other similar buckets sat, nested, on the counter.

He opened a cupboard and took out a box of Wheaties. "What are the buckets for?"

"Cherries," his grandmother said.

"Cherries?"

"Remember that ladder work I said I needed you for? Well, the cherry U-pick orchards open today."

Seth got a bowl out of another cupboard and milk from the refrigerator. He sat down at the table. "But you have to be twelve to go up the ladders."

Grandma Claire peered at him over her shoulder, eyes twinkling. "That's your mother's rule."

Seth felt a pleasant buzz course through him. He'd picked cherries at the U-pick before with his family, but the last couple of years he'd declined to participate because—as he'd told his parents—picking from the ground is kid stuff.

"We leave as soon as you're finished with breakfast," his grandmother said.

Seth had never eaten a bowl of cereal so fast.

THE NEAREST CHERRY U-PICK was at a sprawling, multi-variety cherry orchard in Garden Valley off a gravel lane that ended at the bank of the South Umpqua River. Several vehicles were already parked along the lane, and pickers of all ages, shapes, and sizes swarmed the trees like bees collecting pollen.

U-pick opening day was a much-anticipated event for cherry lovers, and for many it was a family affair. Kids with small buckets bopped around under the trees, excitedly plucking the low-hanging fruit from pliant limbs, jumping in place on their coil-spring legs to snatch every cherry they could reach. The adults and older siblings worked higher in the trees, some from the ground and others balanced on the steps of the three-legged orchard ladders.

Seth's grandmother parked the car and they got out. Seth retrieved the buckets from the car's trunk. "What kind of cherries do you want, Grandma?"

"I want some Bings, some Rainiers, and some pie cherries," she said. She glanced around as if sizing up the situation. "Let's start with the pie cherries. There aren't as many pie cherry trees, so they're likely to be stripped first. Also, they're smaller trees,

so I can keep my feet on the ground where they belong. You'll have to pick the Bings—that's almost all
ladder work."

"I can handle it," Seth said, suddenly feeling a few
inches taller.

The orchard was sectioned by variety. They went
to the pie cherry trees and found one that wasn't
ringed with pickers and still had plenty of fruit
hanging in red clusters from its branches. "When
our buckets are half full," his grandmother said,
"we'll combine them into one bucket and then move
on to the Rainiers. We'll save the Bings for last because by then I'll be tuckered out, and I can stand
ladder watch while you pick."

Seth could have picked faster, but he was enjoying himself too much to hurry. It was so great being
outdoors under the broad expanse of sky, the breeze
from the river caressing his neck, and the earth's
perfume filling his nostrils. Even so, it didn't take
them long to pick their quota of pie cherries.

The Rainier trees were taller than the pie cherry
trees. Grandma Claire picked from the ground while
Seth picked from one of the shorter orchard ladders.
Before he went up the ladder, she gave him a primer
on ladder safety: "Keep both feet on the same rung
while picking. Keep your feet apart, with your weight
centered between the rails. You can reach to the side
to pick, but don't lean more than half your body beyond the rail. If the fruit is out of safe reach, move
the ladder."

"Got it," Seth said and headed up the ladder with
his bucket. He did his best to follow his grandmother's advice. All the same, it took him awhile to

settle his feet properly on the rungs, and a time or two he lost his balance when he reached out too far to the side. But by the time they got to the Bing trees, which were taller and required taller ladders to reach the high-hanging fruit, he felt as confident picking from a ladder as a squirrel does flitting among the branches of a walnut tree.

The orchard attendant weighed their heaping buckets. Seth's grandmother paid for the cherries, and they loaded their bounty into the trunk of the car. Before closing the trunk lid, each of them grabbed a handful of fruit. They stood there eating cherries and spitting the pits onto the ground.

"What are you going to do with all the cherries, Grandma?"

"Give them away"—she laughed—"if we don't eat them all first. And I'll want your help with that too."

She wasn't kidding. When they got back to her apartment, they parceled out the cherries into one-quart storage bags. Then they packed the bags into cardboard boxes and loaded them into the car. They spent the rest of the day delivering cherries to members of his grandmother's quilting group.

"A lot of these ladies aren't able to get out and about on their own," she explained. "So this is something I can do for them. Also, it's a good way to socialize."

She was right about that. Each delivery involved handing over the cherries followed by a minimum fifteen-minute gabfest. Seth remembered some of the women from having attended quilting night, and they greeted him as if he were a long-lost grandson, which was kind of embarrassing.

But all in all, it was a fun day.

"Now aren't you glad you came to stay with me?" his grandmother said as she drove them back to her apartment.

Seth stammered, sensing a trap. "Do I have to answer?"

15

THE NEXT AFTERNOON, the fifth day of Seth's banishment, his dad showed up at the apartment. Seth dared to hope that his dad had come to rescue him.

No such luck.

"I just stopped by to see how things were going," his dad said.

"You mean I can't come home yet?"

"Hey," his grandmother said, "and miss out on all the fun we're having?"

Seth's dad laughed.

Deflated, Seth sagged down onto the living room sofa.

His dad sat down next to him. "There *is* something I want to tell you, though. It's about Henry Garber."

That got Seth's attention. It got Grandma Claire's attention too; she had a curious look on her face as she eased herself down onto her bentwood rocker.

"I got a call from Deputy Waller," Seth's dad said. "He said that the medical examiner has ruled Mr. Garber's death an accidental drowning."

Seth turned that bit of news over in his mind. Accidental drowning? How could that have happened? The water wasn't that deep. Even *he* had survived a plunge into the pond. He shook his head. "And he's the one who told us to be careful not to drown ourselves."

"Sadly," his dad said, "these things happen."

Another thought came to Seth, one that excited him. "Dad, if Mr. Garber's death was an accident, then that means he wasn't murdered. So there's no danger in me coming home, or in me and Collin going down to the pond."

His dad looked doubtful. "I don't know about that. I'll have to talk to your mother. She might agree. But let's not press her on it. It's always better when she comes to her own conclusions."

"Sure, Dad," Seth said, disappointed but not wanting to press the issue with his dad either.

His dad gave him a pat on the knee. "But there's something else I have to tell you, and I think you'll be happy to hear it."

Seth perked up.

"I talked to my friend at the VA hospital like you asked me to. He didn't know anything about Henry Garber beyond what showed up in a search of the VA records. But he put me in touch with someone who advocates for local veterans. He's called an ombudsman. His name is Sam Harris and he was very helpful.

"Mr. Harris made some inquiries and confirmed that, as an honorably discharged veteran—Navy, I think he said—Henry Garber is entitled to military burial benefits. What's more, since Mr. Garber's next of kin can't be located, the VA—with prompting from Mr. Harris—has agreed to take responsibility for the disposition of his body. They'll see to it that his cremated remains get a proper committal in the national cemetery here in town, including a memorial service performed by a VA chaplain, complete with military funeral honors."

"Military funeral honors? What's that, Dad?"

"It means that a military honor guard will attend the service and perform a series of ceremonial acts in honor of a fallen comrade. It will include a gun salute, the playing of 'Taps,' and the folding and presentation of an American flag."

"That's great news, Dad," said Seth. Then a dark thought struck him. "But if the VA can't locate any of Mr. Garber's family, who'll attend the service?"

His dad's eyes went vacant. "I don't know. I didn't think to ask about that."

"Can we go?" Seth blurted without thinking about the implications of what he was asking. "At least that would be someone."

"I'm not sure that would be appropriate, son," his dad said, seemingly taken aback by the notion. "We didn't even know the man. Plus, the service is to be held the day after tomorrow, a workday for me."

But Seth refused to let go of the idea. It didn't matter that they hadn't known Mr. Garber. What mattered was that someone—anyone—showed up at his memorial service. "Grandma can take me," he said. He looked at Grandma Claire for her response. Her eyes were round and her face pale, but she didn't say anything.

"*Please*, Grandma," he said. "I know you didn't

like Mr. Garber, but what does that matter now?"

His grandmother's countenance colored. "I never said I didn't like him. I said—" She shook her head. "Oh, never mind."

They were quiet for a time. Then Seth's dad spoke up. "On second thought, Mom, he does have a point. There's no sense in holding a memorial service if no one attends. And Mr. Garber was a neighbor, however aloof. Maybe it isn't such a bad idea for someone from the family to be there."

Grandma Claire remained tight-lipped as she tipped slowly back and forth in her rocker. When she finally responded, Seth was certain she was going to say no. She surprised him.

"If that's what you really want, Seth," she said in a voice as soft and dry as the sound of rustling leaves, "then I'll take you."

"And Collin? Can he come too?"

She nodded. "If it's okay with his parents."

Seth walked with his dad out to the newly paved parking lot. No stall lines had been painted and cars were parked haphazardly. "Thanks, Dad, for talking to that veterans om . . . om . . . ."

"Ombudsman."

"Yeah, him."

His dad ruffled his hair. "It was only because of your encouragement. I'm proud of you for caring so much."

"Are you sure you can't come to the memorial service?"

"I'll try, son. I'll try."

16

SETH WAS RIGHT: almost no one showed up at the memorial service for Henry Thomas Garber. Seth was there with his grandmother, who seemed unusually preoccupied. And Seth's dad had arranged his work schedule at the last minute so he could attend. Seth's mom, according to his dad, had "respectfully declined" to come to the service, which Seth took to mean that she hadn't thrown anything at him when he asked if she cared to join them.

Seth wished that Collin could have come along, but Collin's mother wouldn't let him. "She thinks it's creepy to mourn the death of some old man you didn't know," Collin had told him over the phone. He didn't say as much, but Seth knew that his friend felt the same way.

Seth saw it differently. He wasn't going to the memorial service to mourn Mr. Garber's passing. It was simply a matter of respect. No one's death should go unacknowledged.

He was glad that his dad had managed to get off work. Grandma Claire's mood brightened as well

when she found out he would be attending the service and was willing to drive. Seth was surprised she
hadn't backed out at that point. "A promise is a
promise," she said. "I said I'd go, and I will."

The Roseburg National Cemetery was located on
the sprawling grounds of the Roseburg VA Healthcare System. "This area used to be a golf course for
veterans," Seth's dad remarked as he turned onto
the lane leading into the cemetery.

It was Seth's first visit to the national cemetery,
and even though this outing was his idea, he felt a
bit uneasy about it. That's because he didn't quite
know what to make of cemeteries. Sure, he knew
that they were where you buried dead people or
locked their ashes away in vaults. But whenever he'd
gone with his family to visit his grandfather's grave
at Roseburg Memorial Gardens, with its matrix of
decaying headstones and plot markers, the place
had seemed eerily empty. If it was populated by the
souls of those laid to rest there, he hadn't sensed it.
All he'd felt in the midst of the heavy silence was a
depressing loneliness.

They crossed a bridge over a small pond populated by ducks and entered the grounds of the national cemetery. Off to the right, a walking path led
to a tall flagpole where an American flag wavered in
the breeze.

From there, the drive looped around an expansive
green. Embedded in the manicured lawn on either
side of the drive were white marble headstones of
similar size and shape. They stood erect in evenly
spaced rows, as if the soldiers buried beneath them

had lined up in final roll-call formation. Most of the cemetery's lawn area, however, remained vacant. Seth commented on this.

"That's because this is a relatively new cemetery," his dad explained. "It's an extension of the old national cemetery located off Harvard Avenue that reached capacity some time ago. Lots of room for new residents here. Although I'm afraid it will fill up all too soon as we continue to lose veterans of World War II and the Vietnam War." He sighed. "War," he said in a disdainful tone.

Seth was aware of his dad's aversion to war; he'd heard such remarks before. It wasn't that his dad was anti-military. He was just against young men and women being shipped overseas to shed their blood on foreign soil for questionable causes. It was an attitude, Seth knew, that had been passed down from mother to son.

Halfway around the oval drive, they came to the open-air pavilion where the service for Mr. Garber was to take place. Two men stood inside the otherwise unoccupied shelter, talking.

Seth's dad pulled his Taurus in behind the lone vehicle in the parking lane and they got out. As they entered the pavilion, one of the men inside—a stoop-shouldered man with a bald head fringed with tufts of white hair—greeted them with a somber nod. "Welcome," he said and ushered them into the first of three rows of metal benches.

"Are we early?" Seth asked as he sat down between his dad and grandmother.

"Right on time," his dad said.

Seth's heart sank. "I was hoping . . ."

"I know, son. Me too. Maybe someone else will show up yet."

But it seemed unlikely. "At least we're here," Seth said.

In front of them was a display stand draped with an American flag. Seth felt a lump in his throat as he viewed the display. He knew what object the Stars and Stripes blanketed. "There'll be no actual body at the memorial service," his dad had informed him, "but rather an urn containing Mr. Garber's ashes that will be interred following the service."

Seth's attention drifted to a table off to the side. On it sat a bouquet of yellow and white flowers and, next to it, a framed black-and-white photograph of a young sailor in uniform. *Henry Garber?* The photo was somewhat out of focus, making it difficult to distinguish clearly the subject's facial features. Even if he'd known what Henry Garber looked like as a young man, Seth wouldn't have recognized him from this photograph. Was this intentional? *In honoring Henry Garber, we present to you the likeness of any young sailor from any war.*

Seth was still staring at the photograph when the other man inside the pavilion approached. He was a thickset man. He had a jowly face and hair the color of the skin of a russet potato. He was dressed in a dark suit, the jacket unbuttoned, and a burgundy tie. "I'm Chaplain Bowman," he said. "Thank you for coming. We'll get things started soon. The honor guard is running a bit late." He stood aside, head bowed, clutching a leather-bound book.

They didn't have to wait long. Within minutes of the chaplain's greeting, a white van pulled up and parked alongside the pavilion. Four men of differing ages, wearing ill-fitting uniforms of various branches of the military, got out and began off-loading items from the van.

"Are those real rifles?" Seth asked his dad.

"Yes, but they won't use real bullets. It will only sound like it."

Just before the service began, two men came walking across the open expanse of lawn at the north end of the cemetery and entered the pavilion. Seth studied them with heart-thrumming curiosity. *Someone else showed up for the service after all!*

They were both older men, but that was about all they appeared to have in common. One was wearing slacks and a dress shirt with a red-white-and-blue-striped tie. He was clean-shaven except for a thin mustache, and his salt-and-pepper hair was neatly brushed back at the sides. He walked with precision, as if marching in a parade.

The other man hobbled along as if his feet hurt every time they hit the ground. He had an unkempt, dingy white beard and bushy eyebrows. His face was blotchy and pitted. He was gaunt, and his khaki pants and wrinkled Hawaiian shirt hung on him loosely. His belt was too big for his waist, and the extra leather hung down like the tongue of a tired dog. He wore an old-style military cap, the foldable kind. Stitched in red along one side of the cap was the designation VIETNAM VET. The other side was adorned with military pins.

The new arrivals seated themselves in the last row of benches, and Seth had to resist the urge to turn around for another glimpse of them.

The service began with the chaplain asking everyone to stand for the opening prayer. The members of the honor guard were already standing. They had taken up a position in a lawn area off to the side of the pavilion. They stood in a straight line, shoulders thrown back, chests out—although not necessarily beyond their bellies. The three of them with rifles rested the butts of their guns on the ground while keeping a grip on the barrels.

From that point on, the ceremony progressed with mind-numbing ritual. The chaplain, reading from what must have been a handbook for military rites, spoke with as much feeling as the digitized voice of a GPS device. Yet it must not be easy, Seth had to admit, to memorialize in death someone you never knew in life. For it was obvious that the chaplain had never laid eyes on the man whose ashes he'd been charged with giving a "fitting burial."

Seth had been to only one other memorial service—his grandfather Harold's. He was four years old at the time. It took place in a church in town that had a high, arched ceiling and shimmering stained glass windows that made him giddy. Lots of people attended, all with sad faces and soft voices. He didn't recall much about the service though, because he'd fallen asleep early on.

He did his best to stay awake now as the VA chaplain droned on, reading from his script: "Let there be no doubt that Seaman Garber merits his place among those enshrined here in this hallowed ground. He answered his nation's call and served with honor, earning several medals, including the Bronze Star, the Meritorious Service Medal, and the

Purple Heart."

Seth leaned toward his grandmother, who sat quietly with her hands folded in her lap, and whispered to her. "What do you think about that, Grandma?"

"I think he must have been a fine soldier," she replied with a faint smile. But there was an unmistakable look of sadness in her eyes.

"Are you all right, Grandma?"

She reached over and squeezed his hand. "Yes, of course."

"So we are privileged here today," the chaplain said, "to pay tribute to Seaman Garber's service and his sacrifice by bestowing upon him these military honors. Will you please stand for the presentation of honors." He turned to face the honor guard, as did Seth and the other members of the sparse audience.

On the voice commands of their leader, the three men with rifles raised their guns and aimed them at the sky. An ear-piercing blast shattered the stillness. Seth flinched. He went deaf for a moment. As the riflemen recharged their weapons and fired a repeat volley—and then a third—Seth felt an upwelling of conflicting emotions.

Concussive waves still echoed in his ears as a lone bugle began playing the mournful strains of "Taps." There was no actual bugler. The music came from a boom box sitting on the ground next to the leader of the honor guard. By the time the last note sounded, Seth's throat was clogged and his breathing was rapid and shallow. He felt awkwardly sad. Beside him, Grandma Claire wiped tears from her eyes.

"You may be seated," said the chaplain.

"Right shoulder, arms," shouted the leader of the honor guard. The riflemen rested their rifles on their right shoulders. "Column formation forward, march." The riflemen lined up one behind the other and, with their leader alongside them keeping time, marched in single file into the memorial pavilion. One by one, they stowed their rifles in a rack there. Then joining their leader, they took up positions around the flag-draped display stand.

"In life," said the chaplain, "Seaman Garber honored the flag, and now the flag will honor him."

Each member of the honor guard grasped a corner of the American flag. Pulling the flag taut, they lifted it, revealing the cremation urn—a glossy wooden box with an eagle engraved on its front panel.

Seth's response to seeing the urn surprised him. His mind failed to make a meaningful connection between Henry Garber, fisherman, and the contents of the box, so he felt very little.

He watched as the honor guard folded the American flag in half lengthwise, and then again. Then two of the soldiers, alternating folds, worked together to fold the flag into a triangular bundle that showed only white stars on a field of blue. They passed the bundled flag to their leader.

A moment of uncertainty followed as the team leader glanced back and forth between the VA chaplain and those seated in the first row. Then, having made his decision, he walked over and knelt down in front of Seth's grandmother. He held the flag out to her.

She gasped; her back stiffened.

"Ma'am," the kneeling soldier said, "this flag is

presented to you on behalf of a grateful nation as an expression of appreciation for the honorable and faithful service rendered by your loved one."

All eyes were on Seth's grandmother now, and he wondered what she would do. Maybe his dad would bail her out by speaking up and accepting the flag himself. But he didn't. Finally, with the panicked look of someone backed up to the edge of a cliff with no choice but to yield or jump, she reached out and took the flag from the soldier. "Thank you," she said faintly. More tears leaked from her eyes.

The soldier stood at attention and saluted before stepping away.

The chaplain came forward. "This portion of the service is concluded. The interment will take place shortly across the way. You're all welcome to attend."

The two men who'd been sitting in the last row of benches were already walking away. Seth overheard the gimpy one say to the other, "Hank wouldn't have given a rat's ass one way or the other." The comment puzzled him and he wondered who these men were.

His dad apparently shared his curiosity. He approached the chaplain and gestured toward the men. "If you don't mind my asking, who are those two fellows?"

The chaplain smiled. "Why, that's John Hooper and Art Winkelman. John's a volunteer at the VA hospital. Very dedicated. Retired Marine. He seldom misses a memorial service for a fellow vet. The old-timer, the one wearing the garrison hat, is Art Winkelman; U.S. Army, retired. Art lives at Eagle Landing, an apartment complex here on the VA grounds. But come to think of it, I don't recall ever seeing him at any of the memorial services before today."

On the drive back to her apartment, Grandma Claire sat in the front passenger's seat with the bundled American flag in her lap. "What in heaven's name am I supposed to do with this?" she said, holding it out as if it were a fallen cake.

"I don't know, Mom," Seth's dad said. "Sew it into one of your quilts."

"Very funny."

She wasn't the only one unsettled by the memorial service. Seth was glad he'd attended but had come away feeling let down. What bothered him was that the service had been so impersonal. The chaplain had followed the ceremonial script without missing a beat, including an acknowledgement of Henry Garber's fine military record. But at no time had he touched on anything of a personal nature about the man, which left Seth all the more curious about the *life* of the dead man he'd now come to know as Seaman Garber.

Right now, however, another matter was uppermost in his mind. "Dad," he said, poking his head up between the front seats, "can I come home soon?" He glanced at his grandmother for her reaction, but she seemed absorbed by her own thoughts.

When his dad didn't answer right away, Seth sank back in his seat, his hopes flagging.

"I have to go back to work," his dad finally said. "But how about I pick you up on my way home this afternoon? I think your mother will be happy to see you."

Seth could hardly contain his glee, but he didn't want his grandmother to feel slighted. "Is that okay with you, Grandma?"

"I guess I'll survive," she said. Then she turned around in her seat and winked at him, and that made him feel better.

17

TWO DAYS AFTER SETH returned home, his mother lifted the log pond ban. "If that man's death really was an accident," she said, "then I guess there's no harm in you boys playing there." Then she put her hands on her hips the way she always did when issuing an edict. "But stay off the water. Leave the rafting to Huck Finn."

Seth was convinced that his mother's change of heart had less to do with her altered thinking about the dangers lurking at the pond and more to do with her not wanting him and Collin constantly underfoot. After Seth's return from exile, the log pond still being off-limits, the boys had spent most of their time hanging around Seth's house playing video games in the den, shooting hoops in the driveway, and dashing in and out of the kitchen to refuel on snacks and sweet drinks.

"They're like hamsters in a ball rolling around the house all day," Seth's mother complained during dinner that second evening after Seth's return.

Baylie piped up. "Mia's brother had a hamster. It

got out of its ball." She scrunched up her face. "Their cat ate it."

Seth drank from his glass of milk and kept quiet.

"They're boys, Laura," his dad said. "They have energy to burn off."

Later that evening, his mother called off her pond ban.

This turn of events should have brightened Seth's spirits, and that first day back at the pond *was* fun for a while. Seth rose early that morning, eager to start the day. The boys had agreed to meet at the watchman's shack as soon as they'd finished their morning chores. Seth dressed, scarfed down his cereal, and got busy. He scattered pellets and grit in the chicken run, and watched as the hens rushed around gobbling up the tidbits. He filled their water bowls. Then he gathered eggs from the nests in the henhouse, placing them in a carton he'd brought for that purpose, and took them into the kitchen.

His mother's head was halfway inside the oven. "So much for self-cleaning," she grumbled.

Seth put the eggs in the refrigerator. "Anything else you want me to do, Mom?"

"Oh—hi, sweetie," she said, withdrawing her head. She blew a wisp of hair out of her face. "Yes. I'd like you to pick some green beans." She pointed at a bowl on the counter. "That should hold all I need."

Bowl in hand, Seth headed out to the vegetable garden. In no time, he was back with a full container. "Anything else, Mom?"

"No. You're free."

Seth bolted for the front door.

His mother's voice chased after him. "Don't forget what I said. You boys—" He was already out the door.

Feeling the thrill of anticipation, he hustled across the pasture. He was about to reclaim the joy of summer. Already the unblinking sun had warmed the earth and awakened the critters of the field. Responding to Seth's footfalls, grasshoppers catapulted from the tall grass and flew to safety. Field mice scampered back to their burrows. A bush rabbit shot from its grassy hideout and darted into a huckleberry thicket. As Seth scaled the fence around the pond, a blue jay sitting on a nearby fencepost squawked at him before swooping away.

Seth wasn't surprised to find Collin already at the pond. Actually, it was Collin's shoes and socks he found first, scattered like a trail of breadcrumbs from the watchman's shack down to the water's edge.

He skittered down the embankment to where Collin crouched in the shallows, pant legs rolled up to his knees, gazing fixedly into a cluster of reeds.

"What is it?" Seth asked.

Collin held up his hands in a call for quiet.

Seth stood still. The quiet lasted several seconds.

Ribbit!

Collin pointed. "There—the biggest bullfrog you ever saw." Muddy water swirled around his ankles as he crept forward. "And I'm gonna catch him."

Seth knew enough about bullfrogs to know that catching one was easier said than done. Plenty of them inhabited the pond. Although they broadcast their presence with loud croaking, they were experts at hiding in the shallows. Also uncannily alert, they leaped out of reach at the slightest hint of danger. Then they would dive under water and, because they could breathe through their skin, stay submerged for a long time.

But Seth could see that his friend was on a mission and he didn't want to discourage him. He had an inspiration. "You catch the frog and I'll nab some grasshoppers to feed it."

Collin inched toward his prey. "Deal."

Seth found an empty jar in the watchman's shack. He scurried back to the pasture and set about capturing grasshoppers, which was only slightly less challenging than catching a bullfrog.

When he was convinced that he'd snagged enough grasshoppers to satisfy even the biggest and hungriest of frogs, Seth headed back to the pond. He got there just in time to see his friend make a diving grab that resulted in a face plant in the mire.

"Gotcha!" Collin cried. He got up, his front side seeping muddy water, and slogged onto the bank with a big bullfrog in his grasp. "We need string," he said, his broad smile revealing threads of moss in his teeth.

Seth used his pocketknife to cut off a strand of fishing line caught in some brambles nearby.

Collin extended one of the frog's back legs. "Tie the line around it."

Seth balked.

"It won't hurt him," Collin said. "And we gotta keep him from getting away while we feed him."

Reluctantly, Seth wrapped the fishing line around the frog's leg, but not too tightly, and tied a double knot.

"Now tie the other end of the line around my wrist."

Seth complied.

Collin set the frog on the ground. It immediately jumped, but only as far as the fishing line allowed.

Collin chuckled. "This is gonna be good." He held out his hand. "Give me a grasshopper."

Seth shook a grasshopper out of the jar and handed it to him. "It'll hop away as soon as you let it loose."

"No it won't," Collin said and casually snapped off the spindly part of the grasshopper's back legs.

Seth winced. "Ohhh!"

"It's all right," Collin said. "Insects don't feel pain like people do. And he's a goner anyway." He set the grasshopper down on the ground several inches in front of the frog. It fluttered its wings and kicked its partial legs but didn't get far.

Nothing else happened right away. Then, so quickly Seth almost didn't see it, the frog's tongue unfurled, glommed onto the grasshopper like fly-paper, and—*gulp!*—curled back into the frog's mouth, the tasty morsel tucked inside. Tasty to a frog, any-way.

Collin cheered. "Wow! I gotta see that again."

Seth coaxed another grasshopper out of the jar and gave it to him.

They fed the frog six grasshoppers, each time marveling at the lightning speed of the frog's whip-like tongue as it reeled in its snack. By then, even Collin was bored with the show.

Seth cut the fishing line from the frog's leg. Three big hops and it was back in the water, swimming away. He dumped the rest of the grasshoppers onto the ground.

"Now what?" Collin said.

"You got mud on your face," Seth said. "That's what."

Collin swiped at his face with the back of his hand and examined the result. "Yep." He went to the edge of the pond and scooped up some muck, which he used to finger paint brown streaks down Seth's cheeks. "So do you," he said, laughing.

Seth returned the favor. Collin followed suit.

Soon their entire faces were masked with mud.

"You look like a savage," Seth told his friend.

Collin stood tall and puffed out his chest. "Me great hunter."

Seth picked up on his friend's thinking. "What are we hunting today?"

"Wild boar."

"Club or spear?"

"Spear."

And on the hunt the boys went. Brandishing spears cut from saplings, they rushed along the network of deer trails around the pond, pretending to track wild boars, although neither of them had ever seen a wild boar except on television.

For Seth, the game quickly got old. He pitched his spear into the brush. "Enough hunting for one day." He made his way down to the pond and washed the mud off his face.

Collin jabbed his spear into the bank. "What do you want to do now?"

"I don't know," Seth said, drying his face with the tail of his T-shirt. Truth was, he didn't feel like doing much of anything else. He sat down on the bank with his elbows on his knees and his chin in his hands and stared at nothing in particular.

"What's with you today? You sick or something?"

"I'm not sick," Seth said, "I'm just—"

"Just what?"

But Seth didn't know what. He only knew that he wasn't having all that much fun on his first day back at the pond. He didn't know why. Maybe it was because it was so hot. Maybe it was because he was still concerned that he'd hurt his grandmother's feelings by not wanting to stay with her any longer in town. Maybe it was something as simple as the depressing sight of their raft, still snagged on the branch, floating uselessly on the water. Or maybe, just maybe, returning to this place made it all too real for him that he would never again see Mr. Garber in his boat out on the pond with his dog at his side.

"I'm just tired, I guess."

Collin pulled his spear out of the ground and heaved it in a rainbow-arched throw into the pond. "That's okay. I'm hungry anyway. Let's go to my house and raid the refrigerator."

"Sure—why not?" Seth said. "But aren't you forgetting something?"

"What?"

"You're a savage."

"Oh—right." Collin splashed pond water on his face and mopped the muddy residue with the sleeves of his T-shirt. He clasped Seth's hands and pulled him to his feet, then laughingly half-carried him the first few feet up the slope.

They climbed on up the bank and headed around the rim of the pond toward Collin's house. They didn't get far before something stopped them in their tracks.

"That's weird," Seth said, peering down the embankment at a small clearing at the water's edge. Yellow police tape, hanging swag-like from the surrounding brambles, outlined the clearing. "Why would the police . . .?" Then it came to him. "That must be Mr. Garber's private boat launch. The deputy said they found it."

"We should go see," Collin said.

"I thought you were hungry."

"I am," Collin said, "so let's not waste time standing here." As if propelled by the magnetic pull of his curiosity, he veered off the path and headed down the brushy slope.

Uh-oh. Here we go again! "Don't cross the tape," Seth hollered. He scrambled after his friend, doing his best to track Collin's zigzag course through the brush.

Upslope from the clearing, Collin stopped outside the ring of yellow tape. Seth caught up with him.

"No boat here," Collin noted.

As Seth gazed around, he recalled what Deputy Waller had said about his men finding Garber's rowboat floating among the reeds along the eastern shore. "It must have drifted farther down," he said, "but this is definitely where it was launched from. Check out the footprints the deputy mentioned."

The footprints—trailing to and from the shoreline—were still clearly visible. Fixed in the recently sun-dried soil, they looked as if they'd been cast in concrete.

Seth studied the pockmarks. "The deputy said they found footprints that weren't Mr. Garber's—or ours."

"So whose are they?"

Seth thought it but didn't say it: *The last person to see Mr. Garber alive.*

18

SETH'S DAD RETRIEVED his router bit case from a storage drawer in his workshop. "I don't understand your continued interest in Mr. Garber, son."

It was Saturday morning and Seth was with his dad in his workshop, where he spent much of his spare time doing woodworking. He made cabinets and counters, bookcases and benches, signs and stools, and pretty much anything else that can be crafted from wood. It was a skill he'd learned from Seth's grandfather Harold.

Seth admired his dad's handicraft and enjoyed watching him work. Sometimes his dad let him operate one of the machines—the table saw or planer or drill press—but only while wearing ear and eye protection, and with his dad closely supervising.

But today wasn't one of those days. Seth had come to the shop with something else on his mind.

"It's hard to explain, Dad. It just still bothers me that Mr. Garber's death has gone so unnoticed—by everyone except us, I mean. It's nice that he got a memorial service and all, and we were able to attend.

But that doesn't seem like enough"—he searched for the right word—"recognition."

"Recognition?"

"Yeah. I mean, Mr. Garber lived alone all those years, and then he died alone. And now it's like we're the only ones who know he ever existed."

His dad chose a bit and took it over to his router table. "That does seem to be the case, and it *is* regrettable. But I don't see that there's anything we can do about it."

"Maybe there isn't," Seth said. "But someone must know something about Mr. Garber. He grew up somewhere, went to school somewhere, worked somewhere. He must have had friends and family at one time. There has to be someone out there who cares about him, someone who'd want to know about his death."

His dad cranked up the router until its collet was accessible and inserted the bit. "I'm sure you're right, son. But neither the VA nor the police have been able to locate any of his family or anyone else with whom he had close ties. Where else is there to turn?"

Seth had a suggestion, one he'd been thinking about for a while. "What about that old soldier who came to the memorial service? Art something. He might know something about Garber's past."

"Why would you think that?"

"Because I heard him refer to Mr. Garber as 'Hank.' Isn't that a nickname for Henry?"

"I suppose it is."

"Friends use nicknames for each other, right? So

this Art something must have been Henry Garber's friend."

His dad rubbed the back of his neck. "Could be. But even if you're right, someone from the sheriff's office probably spoke with him already. And if they'd learned anything useful, they would have followed up on it."

"But can't we go talk to him anyway? The chaplain said he lives right there on the VA grounds."

His dad sighed. "I don't see it doing any good," he said, his voice veering toward impatience.

"Please, Dad. Like you're always telling me and Baylie: *You don't know until you've tried.*"

His dad fell silent then, and the silence was like the reservoir of quiet that follows the tolling of church bells. When he spoke again, it was in a mellower tone. "Well, I don't suppose it would hurt anything if we talked to this Art fellow."

"Great! Thanks, Dad. Can we go today? This afternoon?"

His dad shook his head and laughed. "Give an inch . . ."

THREE-THIRTY THAT AFTERNOON, they knocked on the door of a first-floor apartment at Eagle Landing on the grounds of the Roseburg VA Healthcare System. On the third knock, the door cracked open and a grizzled, bearded face came partially into view.

"If you're sellin', I ain't buyin'," a gruff voice said. Other, hollow sounding voices could be heard in the background.

"Mr. Winkelman?" Seth's dad asked.

The door opened a few more inches. The old man

regarded them through squinty eyes, his eyebrows sticking up like raised hackles. "Maybe."

Seth's dad introduced himself and Seth, then said, "We saw you at Henry Garber's memorial service. We got your name and address from Chaplain Bowman. Could you possibly spare us a few minutes of your time?"

The old man stared at them unblinkingly. Just when Seth thought he was about to shut the door in their faces, Winkelman said, "I reckon I've got nothing better to do at the moment." With that, he dissolved back inside, leaving the door ajar.

The door opened onto a small living room. They entered to find the old man sitting in an overstuffed chair, legs outstretched, elbows resting on the chair's swollen arms, one hand holding a TV remote control. A strand of smoke curled up and over his right shoulder, its source a smoldering cigarette butt mingled with others in an ashtray sitting on a side table next to the chair, which explained the pungent odor of tobacco smoke permeating the air.

Another object, one that Seth recognized, lay on the table as well—the pin-studded military cap Winkelman had worn to Mr. Garber's memorial service. The cap, Seth noted now as he observed the man's bare head, had covered limp strands of thinning gray hair.

"Sit if you'd like," he told them, nodding at a curved loveseat that reminded Seth of a giant padded clamshell. He aimed the remote control at a flat screen TV sitting on a corner stand. The hollow voices emanating from it hushed and the screen blacked out like a burning candle blown out in the dark.

"I hope we're not interrupting a favorite show," Seth's dad said as the two of them sat down on the clamshell.

"Noise," the old man said. "That's all." He set the remote control on the side table. "You were saying . . ."

"We understand that you might have been a friend of Henry Garber's," Seth's dad said.

Winkelman's eyes roamed the room's bare white walls. "I guess you could call Hank a friend of mine," he said. "He wasn't exactly the gregarious type. And I've been known to rub people the wrong way at times myself. But we got along. Though I don't think we were friends so much as kindred spirits. We were fellow survivors."

"Of the war?" Seth's dad said.

Winkelman's gaze turned wooden. "Of the peace."

"I don't understand."

Neither did Seth.

The old man sighed. "Hank Garber had PTSD, a condition I happen to be saddled with also. I met Hank during group counseling sessions here at the VA Mental Health Clinic. Can't say the sessions helped either of us much, but at least it's nice to know you aren't the only one who's crazy."

"What's PT—?" Seth asked.

"PTSD," Winkelman said. "Post-traumatic stress disorder. It's a fancy name for an illness some people get after they've fought in a war or survived some other traumatic event. I guess you could say it's the devil's revenge for all the evil men do to one another."

"And you say that you and Mr. Garber were in

treatment together," Seth's dad said.

Winkelman scratched his scruffy beard with finger-nails that needed trimming. "That's right. We met with a counselor once a week. Six or seven of us, depending on who showed up. But eventually Hank stopped coming. Said the sessions depressed him, which is ironic since depression is what the treat-ment is supposed to help. But Hank said he'd sooner go fishing. Said *that* helped him relax more than anything. So I guess that's what he did."

So that's what brought Mr. Garber down to the pond so often, Seth thought.

"Do you know anything about his personal life?" Seth's dad asked. "Where he came from or anything about his family or other friends?"

Winkelman laughed wryly. "No. One of the things about PTSD is that you tend to feel isolated from everyone and everything. And I think Hank felt that isolation more than most. Whenever the subject of family came up, either in a session or casually, he always clammed up. He never said he had any fam-ily, but he never denied it either, which made me think he had somebody out there somewhere."

"But you don't know who that somebody is or how we can get in touch with them?"

"Haven't the foggiest," Winkelman said. His head lolled back. Moments later, his eyelids drooped as if fatigue—or boredom—had suddenly set in.

They waited to see what would happen. When no-thing changed, Seth's dad stood up. Seth followed his cue.

"We appreciate your talking with us, Mr. Winkel-man," Seth's dad said in a quiet voice, "but I think we've taken up enough of your time."

The old soldier's eyes came slowly open. He glanced over at Seth. "You one of the boys who found Hank's body floating in that old log pond?"

Seth nodded. "Yessir."

The man's eyes flickered. "Well, I don't know what happened out there on that pond," he said, "but I'll tell you this. A sheriff's deputy came to see me after that. When I told him about Hank's depression, he asked me if I thought Hank might have been depressed enough to commit suicide. A fair question, since the suicide rate among people with PTSD is high, and I understand that in Hank's case there were no signs of foul play or a heart attack or anything like that.

"I'll tell you the same thing I told that deputy. I don't believe Hank would have committed suicide, though one member of our therapy group did take his own life last year. And we talked about that in our sessions, and Hank and I talked about it privately. I asked him point-blank if he'd ever contemplated killing himself, because offing myself has crossed my mind more than a few times. And you know what he said? He said that as tempting as suicide sounded sometimes, he wouldn't do it. He wouldn't do it because he still had too much to live for."

Winkelman coughed into his hand several times, then cleared his throat. "Now I don't know what he meant by that, since he had no family around here that I know of. Far as I could tell, he never saw anyone but me and the other emotional cripples here at the VA. But whatever he was referring to, it had a strong enough pull on him to keep him from wanting to end his life."

"That's very interesting," Seth's dad said. Seth thought so too.

"One other thing," Winkelman said, pushing himself up from his chair. He went over to some shelving built into the wall and withdrew a spiral notebook from where it was wedged between two books. He held it up. "As part of our treatment, members of our therapy group were asked to write about our experiences with PTSD. Hank didn't like writing about his illness any more than he liked talking about it. But after being prompted—badgered is more like it—time and again by our counselor, he made one entry in this here notebook. After Hank's death the counselor gave it to me."

He handed the notebook to Seth. "If you really want to know something about Henry Garber and about PTSD, then read what he wrote. When you're finished with it, you can do with it what you will. I don't need it back."

Seth was doing his best to absorb all this new information about Henry Garber, but it was like trying to catch a hundred Frisbees tossed at him at once.

"Thank you," he said as he accepted the notebook.

Winkelman fixed his eyes on Seth. His lips parted as he maintained his stare. "Perhaps I wasn't Hank Garber's only friend after all."

Seth didn't know what to say to that, so he said nothing.

The old soldier sat back down in his chair. It wasn't long before his eyes closed again.

On the drive home, Seth's mind was a jumble of thoughts. Then one separated itself from the others and formed itself into a question. "Dad, if Henry Garber got PTSD from fighting in a war, would that have been the Vietnam War?"

"I imagine so."

"But wasn't that a long time ago?"

"Yes, it was. It began in the mid-1950s, I think, and ended in the mid-70s."

"Then it's been over for"—Seth did some figuring in his head—"more than forty years. Can someone be sick for forty years?"

"When it comes to PTSD, I guess they can."

When they got home, Seth thanked his dad for taking him to see Mr. Winkelman. He held up the notebook the old soldier had given him. "Want to read it?"

"You first," his dad said.

Seth went up to his room and sat down on his bed with Henry Garber's journal on his lap. He fingered the notebook, intending to open it, but something stopped him. Doubt. He was about to read the innermost thoughts of a troubled old man. Was he prepared for that? He was eleven years old. How could he possibly relate, or even understand?

He sat there for the longest time trying to decide what to do. Finally, forcing his doubts aside, he opened the notebook and read Henry Garber's words:

War is an alternate reality. But unlike the alternate realities created in fiction or the movies, which you can escape by closing a book or walking out of a theater, war—once you've participated in its atrocities—stays with you forever. It remains lodged in your head like shrapnel that can't be removed because it's embedded too deeply in your brain.

But it's not ordinary shrapnel. It's not something you can count on to remain inert. Rather, it's like an unexploded bomb that can self-detonate anytime, anywhere. And you have no control over when and where.

War is the alternate reality I've never been able to escape. Why? Because I have a condition called post-traumatic stress disorder, PTSD for short. There are many myths associated with PTSD, the most deceptive of which is that "it's all in your head."

19

SETH DIDN'T HAVE A COMPUTER of his own, so whenever he wanted to play computer games or look something up on the internet, he used his parents' desktop in the den. Before he used it, he had to ask permission. He knew that other kids his age had their own computers, but his parents had insisted that he could have one only when he began middle school.

It wasn't a big deal to Seth. His dad had a laptop that he used mainly for work, and Seth's mom used the desktop only on occasion, to share photos on Facebook or look up recipes. And although Baylie sometimes used the desktop to run learning programs or play games, Seth had never felt deprived of computer time. What's more, he would soon be entering middle school, so the time for him to be allowed his own computer was fast approaching.

"Can I use the computer?" he asked his mom.

"Are you done with your chores?"

"Yes, ma'am."

"Then have at it."

It was the day after Seth and his dad had met with Art Winkelman. Lying in bed the night before, and all that morning as he'd gone about his chores, Seth hadn't been able to stop thinking about the old soldier and the notebook he'd given them.

Seth had read Henry Garber's journal entry several times but didn't fully comprehend what Garber was saying. He understood that PTSD was an illness some people suffer after fighting in a war. But how and why did they suffer? And why did the suffering last so long?

These questions were still with him as he waited for Collin to finish his own chores so they could head out on the adventure they had planned for the day. They were going to ride their bikes on the logging roads in the surrounding hills and look for spotted owls. It was a joke, of course—the looking-for-spotted-owls part. Although thousands of acres of forest in the county had been declared off-limits to logging because of concerns for the loss of spotted owl habitat, no one Seth knew had ever seen one of the creatures.

After getting his mother's permission, Seth sat down at the computer in the den and googled "PTSD." A post on the U.S. Department of Veterans Affairs website caught his eye. He clicked on it and began reading:

What is PTSD?

PTSD (post-traumatic stress disorder) is a mental health problem that some people develop after experiencing or witnessing a life-threatening event, like combat, a natural disaster, a car accident, or sexual assault.

It's normal to have upsetting memories, feel on edge, or have trouble sleeping after this type of event. It may be hard to do normal daily activities, like go to work, go to school, or spend time with people you care about.

He read on with interest, eager to know more about this terrible disorder. What he learned was that PTSD is not a sign of weakness. It can happen to anyone who experiences a traumatic event.

Personal factors like a previous trauma, age, and gender can affect whether a person will develop PTSD. What happens after the traumatic event is also important. Stress can make PTSD more likely, while social support can make it less likely.

He also learned that people with PTSD often have nightmares about the event. Sometimes they even feel as if they are reliving it. This is called a flashback. When the bad memories continue over time, PTSD sufferers can develop feelings of hopelessness, shame, or despair. They can become depressed and anxious. They can have drinking or drug problems, and have trouble holding a job or maintaining relationships.

PTSD, the VA site went on to say, can be treated with medication and counseling. Sometimes the treatment helps people get rid of the symptoms. But for some people, even with treatment the symptoms never go away.

When he finished reading the article, Seth printed it out and went up to his room. The idea that a person could suffer for a lifetime after experiencing a traumatic event was new to him, and more than a little unsettling. It seemed so unfair. He was rereading the article on PTSD when he heard his mother call up the stairs, "Seth, Collin is here."

"Come on up, Collin," he hollered back.

"I know about PTSD," Collin said after Seth told him about the meeting with Art Winkelman and showed him Henry Garber's journal. "My dad's uncle had it. My dad said that it was just his excuse for not being able to keep a job. Some guys coming back from a war, he said, only pretend they're messed up in the head so they can get disability benefits from the government."

Seth was quick to respond. "I don't think Henry Garber was pretending. Besides, according to what I read about PTSD, you can get it from things other than fighting in a war. You can get it from something scary or awful that happens to you, like . . . you know, bad stuff."

"You mean," Collin said flippantly, unaware of the weight of his words, "like finding a dead body floating in a pond."

That's exactly what Seth meant.

20

IN THE ROBERSON HOUSEHOLD, one rule above all others was not to be broken. Winter or summer, spring or fall, school days or weekends, good weather or bad, unless Seth was excused "for just cause" (his mother's words), he was to be home by 5:30 p.m. for the family dinner, served promptly at six o'clock. It was a tradition passed down through generations of the Roberson family, and Grandma Claire, even after moving to town, often joined them around the dinner table.

Usually it wasn't a problem for Seth to be home in time for dinner, though on occasion he had to dash back from an outing so as not to be late. It was easy to lose track of time when you were having fun. He wore a watch but didn't always remember to check it.

Collin had no such time constraints on him. His dad worked irregular hours, often far from home, and his mom didn't much like to cook, so the family seldom sat down to dinner together. It wasn't surprising, then, that whenever Collin was invited to stay for dinner at Seth's house he gladly accepted, and his mother readily consented.

So it was that the Robersons, including Grandma Claire, plus Collin, sat around the dinner table enjoying a meal of pot roast and potatoes, gravy made from the drippings, carrots and onions, and homemade biscuits.

"What have you boys been up to today?" Seth's dad asked as he spooned gravy onto his potatoes.

"We went up into the hills to look for spotted owls," Collin said.

Seth's dad laughed. "You'd be more likely to find Bigfoot."

"I hope you watched out for logging trucks," Seth's mother said. "Those drivers come down those narrow mountain roads like they're racing in the Indy 500."

"We saw a dead deer on the road," Seth said. "But no dead kids on bikes."

"Not funny," said Grandma Claire.

"I thought it was funny," Baylie said.

"You would," Seth said.

"What did you do today, Baylie?" Seth's grandmother asked.

"Mom and I went shopping for school clothes."

"That sounds fun."

"It should sound expensive," Seth's mother said. "Because that's what it was. I can't believe how much kids' clothes cost these days."

"You get better deals at Goodwill," Collin said, then he stuffed his mouth with enough roast beef to choke a mountain lion. His next words were barely intelligible: "That's where my mom gets all my school clothes."

Seth's mother glanced at her mother-in-law. "I'll have to keep that in mind."

Seth knew the reason for the look. Grandma Claire occasionally shopped at Goodwill for quilting cloth. One day she'd made an offhand suggestion that Seth's mother might find some clothes for the kids there. His mother took exception to the idea. "I'll not have my kids wearing someone else's hand-me-downs," she said.

"I was only talking about playclothes," his grandmother said. "You said yourself that they wear them out so fast."

But Seth's mother wouldn't hear of it, and Grandma Claire never raised the issue again.

Seth was sorry the subject had come up and was glad when conversation was interrupted by the ringing of the telephone.

"I'll get it," Seth's dad said. He got up from the table and headed into the living room.

"If it's Doris," Seth's mother called after him, "tell her I'll phone her back. She should know not to call during dinnertime."

After taking the call, Seth's dad came back into the dining room, a distracted look on his face.

"Who was it, dear?" Seth's mother asked.

"It wasn't Doris," he said, returning to his seat.

"Who was it then?"

He sipped from his water glass. "An attorney."

"An attorney?" Seth's mother said. "What attorney?"

"An attorney from town named Charles Banks."

"What did he want?"

"To schedule a meeting."

"With who?"

"With us."

"Us? You mean you and me?"

Seth's dad nodded. "Yes, he wants to meet with us in his office tomorrow morning at ten o'clock. Said it was important. I'll have to juggle my work schedule."

Seth's mother frowned. "But why does he want to meet with us?"

His dad picked up his fork. Then he set it back down. He stared at his plate. "Well, it's a curious thing. Evidently, the late Henry Garber left a will—one that this attorney, Mr. Banks, drew up for him a year or so ago. Banks says he wants us to attend a reading of the will."

"What's a will?" Baylie asked.

"It's a document," their dad replied, "a piece of paper that tells what a person wants done with his property—his belongings—when he dies."

Seth's mother shook her head. "I still don't understand. What did we have to do with Mr. Garber that would call for us to be present at a reading of his will? And why hasn't this come up before now? Shouldn't the police have known about the will? Shouldn't all this have already been taken care of?" She had a habit of asking multiple questions at once.

As always, Seth's dad did his best to answer her flurry of questions. "Banks said he only recently found out about Garber's death. He was out of town when the body was discovered. The sheriff's office didn't know about the will because their officers didn't find a copy when they went through Garber's belongings. The attorney has since provided them with one. As to why he wants us to attend the reading of the will, he said he'd explain that when we meet with him tomorrow."

As Seth listened to his parents' conversation, an exciting prospect entered his mind. "Dad, if Mr. Garber left a will, wouldn't it say who he left his property to? And that would probably be a close friend or relative, right? Then they'd be notified, and they'd find out that he died. They would be sad, but at least they'd know—and that would be a good thing."

"That's right, son, assuming the named beneficiary—that is, the person or persons he willed his property to—is alive and can be found."

"Oh, I hope that's the case," Seth said. "It would mean that there's someone out there who cares about Mr. Garber, or at least he cared enough about *them* to name them his ben . . . ben . . ."

"Beneficiary," his dad said. "Yes, but don't get your hopes up too much. Some people, particularly those with no family or close friends, will their property to entities other than people—to a church, for instance, or some other nonprofit organization."

"I'll bet the old man left everything to his dog," Collin said. "I heard about this crazy old lady who died and left a million dollars to her cat." He laughed. "What would a cat do with a million dollars?"

But Seth's mother wasn't laughing, and she wasn't done voicing her opinion. "I still don't see what any of this has to do with us. It's like we're being dragged into that old man's affairs just because the boys found his . . . well, it's wrong, and I don't like it."

Seth's dad reached for a biscuit. He broke it apart and buttered it. "I think we'll just have to wait and see what the attorney has to say, dear. But I'm thinking this meeting must have something to do with the authorities' inability to locate Mr. Garber's next of kin. That leaves us."

Seth's mother scowled. "What do you mean *that leaves us?*"

"I mean, I'm guessing that Banks found out we attended Henry Garber's memorial service. In his eyes, that makes us interested parties."

"I didn't attend any memorial service," Seth's mother snapped. "And I'm certainly not an *interested party*. So why does he want me there?"

Seth's dad shrugged. "Perhaps he's confused the two Mrs. Robersons. What do you think, Mom?"

Grandma Claire wiped her mouth with her napkin, folded it, and placed it next to her plate. "I don't know what to think," she said in a shaky voice.

"Claire, are you all right?" Seth's mother asked. "You look a little peaked."

His grandmother pushed her chair away from the table. "Actually, I'm not feeling all that well. I think I'll go home and lie down."

"Would you like me to drive you, Mom?" Seth's dad asked.

Grandma Claire waved him off. "That won't be necessary. I'll be fine. Probably just indigestion."

Seth's dad walked her to her car.

"Are you sure she's okay to drive?" Seth's mom asked when he returned.

"She seemed well enough. I'll call her later and

make sure she got home okay."

When everyone was finished with the main course, Seth's mother brought out dessert. "Would you like some bread pudding?" she asked Seth's dad.

"I'll pass," he said. "I'd prefer a glass of wine."

"Pour one for me too," she said.

Seth, Collin, and Baylie happily devoured their dessert. When they were done, Seth and Collin helped carry the dinner dishes into the kitchen.

"Set them in the sink," Seth's mother said. "I'll load the dishwasher later."

It was still light outside, so Seth and Collin went out to play Frisbee catch in the backyard. Seth had never fully gotten the hang of tossing a Frisbee. His throws usually sailed wide or fell short, causing Collin to have to run and leap or dive to snag the disk in flight. He didn't seem to mind. It was all part of the fun. He'd whoop and laugh, and when in his opinion he'd made a spectacular grab, he'd strut around like a soccer star who'd just scored a goal.

When the boys tired of tossing the Frisbee, they sprawled on the grass under a black walnut tree. Light was beginning to drain from the sky. The sun would soon be dropping below the crest of the mountains in the west.

Collin scratched at the ground with a stick. "I should be heading home," he said sullenly. Then all at once he sat upright, face beaming. "Hey, how about you come home with me and spend the night."

Seth liked the idea. In the summer, the boys often overnighted at each other's house. But when they went back inside and Seth asked his parents, his dad said, "Not tonight, son. There's something we need you to do in the morning."

"What?"

His dad glanced toward the sofa, where Seth's mother sat with her legs drawn up, reading an issue of *Better Homes and Gardens* magazine. "We'll talk about that in the morning," he said.

"Sorry," Seth told Collin when the boys were back outside.

"That's okay," Collin said, not one to dwell on small disappointments. Seth liked that about his friend.

When Seth went to bed that night, his thoughts kept him from falling asleep right away. He was curious about Mr. Garber's will. Who had the old man left his property to? He hoped it was a living person and not one of those—what had his dad called them?—"entities." He also wondered what his parents needed him to do in the morning.

But that wasn't all that kept him awake. He heard voices coming from his parents' room—his mother's mostly. He couldn't make out her words, but from her tone, he knew that she wasn't happy about something.

21

THE NEXT MORNING AT BREAKFAST, Seth's mother told him, "When you're done eating, I want you to go change clothes. Put on some school clothes."

When dressing that morning, Seth had put on an older pair of jeans—ones that his mother wouldn't make a fuss about if they got torn or muddy—a T-shirt, and last year's sneakers. It's what he always wore on those summer days when he planned to play outside or help his dad with the yard work or hauling firewood or the like.

"School clothes?" he said. "Mom, it's July. There's no—"

"Just do as I say," his mother said.

"I don't have to put on school clothes," Baylie said pertly. "Grandma's taking me to my swim lesson at the Y."

"Bully for you," Seth said.

After breakfast, he went up to his room and changed clothes. When he came back downstairs, his dad was sitting in his recliner in the living room, drinking coffee. "Sit down, son," he said, and Seth did. "Your mother wanted you to change clothes because you'll be going with us this morning to the attorney's office. We'll drop Baylie off at your grandmother's on the way."

Seth reflected on that. The meeting, he understood, was for the reading of Mr. Garber's will. But why was he being included? "Is it because I'm an interested party too?"

His dad smiled. "Come to think of it, I reckon you've been the most interested party from the beginning."

ON THE RIDE TO TOWN, Baylie chattered away as if the only thing happening in the world that day was her going swimming at the Y. "The pool water's warm. It's like a bath. Tallie will be there. Her mom's bringing her. And maybe Chrissy." She bounced up and down in her seat. "It's going to be *sooo* much fun."

"I thought Grandma was sick," Seth said.

"She's better now," Baylie said. "I talked to her on the phone this morning. She said . . ."

Seth tuned his sister out.

At Grandma Claire's, he and his dad stayed in the car while his mom walked Baylie to the apartment. "We don't have to pick her up," she said when she returned. "Claire will bring her home after her swim lesson."

"That's fine," his dad said.

The remainder of the ride was marked by a conspicuous silence that Seth sensed was about more than Baylie's absence.

The lawyer's office was in a storefront downtown,

sandwiched between a brewpub and a secondhand store. Seth's dad parked the car along the street in the closest available space.

They entered the law office through a doorway over which hung a sign that said CHARLES S. BANKS, ATTORNEY AT LAW, LLC. "I'm David Roberson," Seth's dad told a young woman with pink hair and gem-studded eyeglasses sitting behind the reception desk. "We have a ten o'clock appointment with Mr. Banks."

"Please have a seat," the receptionist said. "I'll see if Mr. Banks is ready for you."

He was. They'd hardly sat down when Mr. Banks appeared in a doorway and invited them into his office. He was tall and slender and loose-limbed, like a marionette. He had long, gray-streaked hair tied back in a ponytail. He was dressed in jeans and a knit shirt. Seth had never met a lawyer, but this one didn't resemble the pinstripe-suited, stiff-backed legal eagles he'd seen on television.

The man's office was equally unexpected. It was lined with bookshelves, but they held more pottery than books. And hanging on the wall behind a distressed-wood desk was an enlarged photograph of a man sitting at a potter's wheel, his hands cupped around clay in the shape of a narrow-mouthed, wide-bottomed jug. Seth peered at the man in the photo and then at the man they were meeting with and decided they were one and the same.

Mr. Banks shook hands with Seth's dad, said "pleased to meet you" to Seth's mom, and turned to Seth. "And you must be Seth." He extended a hand.

Seth always felt funny about shaking an adult's

hand. It was as if he'd been handed an object he didn't know what to do with. But he shook the attorney's hand and returned his greeting: "Pleased to meet you."

Mr. Banks gestured for them to sit down in a trio of chairs lined up in front of the desk. "I apologize, Mr. Roberson, if I seemed cryptic over the phone last evening," he said as he seated himself behind the desk. "But I felt we needed to discuss this matter in person."

"You said Mr. Garber left a will?"

"That's right."

"And there will be a reading of the will today?"

"In a manner of speaking."

Seth's dad cocked his head. "I'm afraid I don't understand. Are we here about a will or not?"

"Again, I apologize," said Mr. Banks. "Please allow me to clarify my reason for bringing you all here today."

"That would be appreciated."

The attorney nodded. "A year or so ago, Henry Garber came to me and asked me to draw up his will. He'd been referred to me by the local veterans service office. In the past, I've done pro bono work for veterans. I'm a veteran myself. It was a simple document to draft, so I was happy to do it at no charge." He rested a hand on a file folder lying on his desk. "I have here a copy of Mr. Garber's will, the original of which has been filed with the probate court. My other duty is to determine who's entitled to receive a copy of the will and provide them with one to read."

"But I thought that's why we were here," Seth's

mother said with a touch of annoyance in her voice, "for the reading of the will."

"That's correct," said Mr. Banks. "But, you see, the reading of a will as portrayed on TV and in the movies is a thing of the past, when not everyone could read. Today, with almost universal literacy, the attorney merely sends a copy of the will to each involved party for them to read. But with this will, I thought it best to have you come into my office so I could hand you a copy and go over a few of its key provisions with you."

He withdrew an envelope from the file folder and extended it to Seth's dad. "Mr. Roberson, in this envelope is a copy of the will of Henry Thomas Garber, presented to you and your wife as required by law."

After a moment's hesitation, Seth's dad reached out and took the envelope. He glanced at Seth's mom, whose displeasure with this development was stamped on her face, then opened it. He pulled out the document, unfolded it, and flipped through its pages.

The attorney took up his copy of the will. "As you can see from the declaration at the top of page one," he said, "this is indeed the Last Will and Testament of Henry Thomas Garber. Section One, Paragraph One revokes all prior wills. Skipping down to Paragraph Three, you'll see that I'm named as the executor of the will, with the powers granted to me as listed. Now, if you'll skip to page two. There, in Paragraph One of Section Two, under the heading 'Disposition of Assets,' you'll find the critical information regarding Mr. Garber's wishes for the distribution of his property. I'll let you read that item for yourself."

Seth's dad turned to page two. Seth's mother leaned in beside him as the two of them read the indicated paragraph.

Seth looked on, eager to know who Mr. Garber had left his property to—a friend? a long-lost relative? *Surely not his dog!*

Suddenly his mother gasped. She went rigid. She glared across the desk at Mr. Banks. "This has to be a mistake," she said, shaking her head in disbelief.

The attorney looked at Seth and smiled. "Son, is your name Seth Randall Roberson?"

"Yessir," Seth said.

"And are you the son of David and Laura Roberson, and the grandson of Claire Roberson?"

"Yessir."

"In that case," said Charles Banks, "I don't believe there's been a mistake."

22

"**BUT WHY ON EARTH** would Henry Garber have willed his entire estate to our Seth?" his mother asked, looking dazed.

"That's a question I can't answer," said Mr. Banks. "I met with Mr. Garber twice—once when he came to this office to have me draw up his will, and again when he returned to sign it. On neither visit did he divulge any information other than what was necessary for me to complete the document. When I handed him a copy, he declined it, saying that he already knew what it said."

Seth was confused by the exchange between his mother and the attorney. Had he understood them correctly? It sounded as if, from what they were saying, that in his will Mr. Garber had left all his property to *him*. But could that be true? Was it even legal for a person to leave everything he owned to an eleven-year-old boy? And even if it *was* legal, why would Mr. Garber have done such a thing? Seth hadn't really even known the man. Sure, he'd waved at him whenever he'd seen him at the pond, fishing pole in hand, dog at this side. But it wasn't as if they were friends or anything. Mr. Garber was an old man, and he was just a boy.

"Can I see the will?" he asked, out of raw curiosity.

"I don't see why not," his dad said.

"David, it will only confuse him," Seth's mother insisted.

His dad handed him the document. "It seems to have confused all of us. Besides, he *is* the named beneficiary."

Seth began reading the will, almost immediately getting stuck on words he didn't understand. He handed it back to his dad. "Maybe we can go over it together later."

"I think that's a good idea, son."

The attorney spoke up again. "There's one other provision of the will I'd like to point out. Mr. Garber's estate, as listed in Attachment A, includes miscellaneous personal property, a piece of real estate, and a vehicle, all of which will eventually go to Seth.

"However, in Oregon, a minor—that is, a person under the age of eighteen—cannot own property in his name. Therefore, any titled property such as real estate and vehicles inherited by a minor must be held in trust for that person until they reach the age of majority. Section Three of Mr. Garber's will provides for the creation of such a trust and, furthermore, specifies that the executor is to serve as the trustee. So, as executor, I'll also be acting as the trustee of that trust."

"You mean I get Mr. Garber's house and truck too?" Seth asked, more confused than ever.

"Indeed," the attorney said. "But not until you

turn eighteen. Until then, you'll have the right to use them, but not legal ownership. All that is something we'll have to work out, in consultation with your parents of course."

Seth's mother shook in agitation. "This is crazy. What was that old man thinking?"

The attorney answered in a calm voice. "Again, I can't speak to Mr. Garber's motivation. I can only tell you what his will states and how the law applies."

"I still say that there's been a mistake here," she said, tossing up her hands.

Mr. Banks sat back in his chair and said no more.

It was Seth's dad who, as Seth had seen him do so many times before, intervened to restore order to a chaotic situation. "Thank you, Mr. Banks, for fulfilling your legal duty here today. I think we should go now, and I'll be in touch with you later when we've had a chance to go over the will more thoroughly and digest its contents."

"That will be fine," Mr. Banks replied.

The next instant, Seth's mother had a firm grip on his forearm and was marching him out the door.

The brittle silence inside the car on the ride home was broken only by his mother's occasional clipped outbursts. "I don't get it." "It doesn't make sense." "What could have possessed . . . ?" "Who is this hippie lawyer anyway?" After each eruption, she would shudder and huff and then go quiet until the next outburst. Seth's dad remained mute as he steered the car on the familiar path home.

Seth knew that his mother was upset about Mr. Garber's will, but he didn't understand why, and it worried him that some of her anger might be directed at him.

"Mom," he asked, "did I do something wrong?"

His mother gazed into the backseat, her expression wavering between emotions until it settled on concern. "No, dear. Why would you think that?" Her uneasy smile twitched at the corners.

"Because you're so upset that Mr. Garber left all his property to me."

"I'm only upset because"—she sighed—"because Mr. Garber's bequest to you is so confounding. And it only complicates things for . . . well, for all of us." Then she quickly added, "But it's not your fault, dear. You mustn't think that. Old people do silly things sometimes. But why Mr. Garber chose to name you in his will I simply can't fathom."

Seth felt better knowing that his mother wasn't mad at him. He too was bewildered by his inheritance. And now that he thought about it, it did kind of complicate things. What was he supposed to do with an old house and a neglected pickup truck? He had no idea. There *was one thing* of Mr. Garber's, however, that he longed to have as his own. But this wasn't the time to bring it up.

Back at home, Seth called Collin to tell him the news.

"Cool!" Collin said, with no hint of jealousy. "Weird, but cool. Better than him leaving everything to his dog."

"My mom doesn't think it's cool. She's really mad about it."

"Why?"

"She says it complicates things."

"Hey," Collin said, "I gotta stay home until my mom gets back from her doctor's appointment. But then I'll come over and we can start making plans."

"Plans for what?"

"For what to do with your hillside estate. We'll call it Garberland in honor of the old man. Wow! It'll be like—the best thing ever. You'll have your own kingdom, and I'll be knight of the realm."

Seth appreciated his friend's easy acceptance of his inheritance and his eagerness to make use of it, but he knew that things weren't as simple as Collin made them out to be. "I can't actually own the property until I turn eighteen. It's got to be held in trust, which means the lawyer is in charge of everything for now."

"But it's yours, right? So we can go up there and hang out and not get in trouble."

"My parents may have something to say about that."

"But we can still plan, can't we?" Collin was always keen on planning their next big adventure.

"Sure—why not?" Seth said. "Come on over after your mom gets home."

He had just hung up the phone, when it rang. Thinking it was Collin calling back, he answered it.

"Hi, Seth," a familiar voice said. "This is Deputy Waller. Is your dad home?"

23

"**WHY CAN'T I STAY?**" Seth asked. "This is about Mr. Garber's will, isn't it?"

From the moment he'd found out that Deputy Waller was coming to the house again to talk with his parents, Seth sensed that it was about the newly disclosed will. His parents hadn't said as much, but after the phone call from the deputy, his mother's agitation got the better of her. "This whole situation is so asinine!" she declared and stomped off into the kitchen.

Seth didn't know what asinine meant, but he knew enough to stay out of his mother's way. So did his dad, who put off going to work long enough to meet with the deputy.

By the time Waller arrived, Seth's mother had composed herself enough to join Seth's dad and the deputy in the living room, where she sat stone-faced on the sofa alongside her husband. Now Seth's dad was telling him and Baylie to go to their rooms and stay there until they were told they could come out.

"But Dad—"

"Seth, do as I say."

Baylie was already hopping up the stairs. "Come on, Seth. Let's play a game."

Seth didn't want to play a game, especially not with his sister. She was always dragging out some dumb kid's game, like Guess Who? or Chutes and Ladders, wanting him to play. Sometimes, just to be nice, he'd play with her. But it would get boring fast, and no matter how long they played, she always wanted to play longer. "Go play with your dolls or something," he told her as he shuffled up the stairs.

He went to his room and closed the door with an intentional clunk. A few seconds later, he eased the door open. He crept to the top of the stairwell and crouched down just far enough back so he wouldn't be seen if someone glanced up the stairs. From there, he could hear the words being spoken below.

"I assure you," Seth's dad was saying, "we're as surprised by this as you are."

"And you're saying that you knew nothing of the will before the attorney called you yesterday?"

"That's right," his dad said. "As I told you before, we hardly knew the man. And we knew even less about his affairs. You yourself said that your investigation failed to identify anyone Garber had close ties with."

"That's true," the deputy said. "But I must say, the will casts his death in a new light."

"What new light? The medical examiner's report concluded that there was no evidence of foul play, that the man drowned accidentally—a finding supported by your investigation. How does the will change that?"

"Please understand, Mr. and Mrs. Roberson, that I'm not here to make accusations. But it's my job to resolve any lingering questions about Henry Garber's death. And I think it's reasonable to ask why he chose to name your son as the sole beneficiary of his estate. Normally, a person doesn't leave all his property to someone with whom he has no special connection."

"I understand that," Seth's dad responded. "That's why this is so baffling to us as well. Because other than the occasional casual contact Seth had with him down at the pond, there's no connection we know of to justify Garber's actions."

Seth had yet to hear his mother's voice, but the deputy's next question told him that he was about to.

"Is that the way you see it, Mrs. Roberson?"

Seth's mother wasn't one to mince words and she wasn't about to start doing so now. "I see it," she said, "as the lunacy of a reclusive old man who had no one to leave his property to because he'd cut himself off from anyone and everyone who might have cared about him. Then for some reason—God knows why—he fantasized about having a relationship with our Seth. A wave, a smile from someone who's just being friendly—for some nutcases that's all it takes. All I know is that I don't like it. And I don't like your coming here and asking questions as if you think we, or our son, have done something wrong."

"If that's the impression I've given you, I apologize," Deputy Waller said. "That was not my intent. And you're probably right. Old people, especially ones who have isolated themselves, often do crazy things. This could well be just another example of that."

It went quiet then, and Seth figured the deputy was about to leave. Then he heard him say, "Even so, would you mind if I talked to Seth one more time?"

"*Must* you?" Seth's mother said.

"It'll take only a few minutes, and you can be with him all the while."

When he heard his dad say, "I'll get him," Seth hopped up and scrambled back along the second-floor hallway. Behind him, his dad's voice resonated up the stairwell. "Seth, come down here please."

Seth opened and closed his bedroom door, trying to make it sound as if he'd been inside the whole time. He went to the head of the stairs. "Did you call me, Dad?"

"Yes, son. Come on back downstairs now. Deputy Waller would like to have a word with you."

Baylie materialized at the top of stairs alongside Seth.

"Not you, Baylie," their dad said. "You go on back to your room."

"Do I have to?"

"Just for a little longer, honey."

"Okay, Daddy."

Seth came down the stairs and followed his dad into the living room.

"Sit here," his mother said, patting the sofa cushion next to her. She put an arm around him and pulled him close.

"Good to see you again, Seth," the deputy said. "Is it all right if I ask you a couple of questions?"

Seth squirmed, trying to loosen his mother's embrace. "I guess so."

"Good," Waller said. "Now, am I correct in assuming that you know about Henry Garber's will and its provision that all his property is to go to you?"

"Yessir."

"What do you think about that?"

Seth didn't know what to think about it, and he told the deputy as much.

"You can't think of any reason he would have chosen you as his sole heir?"

Seth had already puzzled long and hard over that question without coming to a logical conclusion. "The only reason I can think of is that he didn't know who else to leave his stuff to."

"But why you? Why not Collin? Or you and Collin?"

Seth could only guess. "Maybe it's because I waved at him whenever he came down to the pond and Collin didn't."

"Did he ever wave back, or come over and talk to you?"

"No, sir. He only spoke to us the one time we already told you about. He came down to the pond one day when Collin and I were wading in the shallows netting tadpoles. I slipped on the muddy bottom and fell on my butt. Mr. Garber must have seen me go down. 'Try not to drown yourselves,' he said, though it was hardly bathwater deep. Then he went off fishing like he always did. Those were the only words I ever heard him speak."

"And yet you continued waving whenever you saw him?"

"Yessir."

"Why?"

Seth hunched his shoulders. "Because that's what you do when you're out and about and you see someone. You smile and wave. It doesn't matter if they smile or wave back. Isn't that right, Dad?"

A smile rippled across his dad's face. "Yes, son."

Deputy Waller stroked his chin. "I can't argue with that. I reckon we'd all do well to follow that example. Thank you, Seth." He stood up. "I apologize for the intrusion, Mr. and Mrs. Roberson, and I thank you for your time."

He was headed for the front door when he stopped and turned around. "By the way, Mr. Roberson, do you think your mother could shed some light on any of this? You mentioned that she lived out here for many years before moving into town. I'd meant to contact her earlier but never got around to it. But now I'm wondering if she might know something about Henry Garber that would help us make sense of things."

"If she does," Seth's dad said, "she's never indicated as much to me. But to know for certain, you'd have to ask her."

"You'd be wasting your time," Seth's mother said, "and I'll tell you why. Before bringing Baylie home earlier today, Claire called here to make sure we were back from the attorney's office. She asked how our meeting went. I told her about Mr. Garber's will—

about his leaving everything to Seth. She was flab-bergasted. She said, and I quote, 'Why in God's name would he have done that?'"

The deputy shrugged. "I guess that's that, then."

24

WHEN THE DAY CAME for the follow-up meeting with Mr. Banks, it was obvious to Seth that his mother still hadn't come to terms with the contents of Henry Garber's will. She hadn't said any more about it in his presence, but her slamming of cupboard doors and banging of pots and pans was telling.

He wasn't surprised when she announced that morning that she wouldn't be attending the second meeting with the attorney. "I'll have nothing more to do with the matter," she said in a steely voice.

Truth be told, Seth was relieved that she wouldn't be accompanying them, and he sensed that his dad felt the same way. Still, his mother's puffed-up condemnation of Mr. Garber troubled Seth. It was as if she believed that the Roberson family had somehow been wronged by the old man's final wishes.

"Are you sure Mom's not mad at me for inheriting Mr. Garber's stuff?" he asked his dad as they drove to town.

"If she's mad at anyone," his dad said, "it's Henry Garber."

But what's the point of being mad at a dead person? Seth wondered.

IN MR. BANKS'S UNLAWYERLY OFFICE, Seth sat and listened as the attorney went over the provisions in the preliminary draft of the trust to be set up to manage Henry Garber's estate. All of Garber's titled assets, he explained to Seth and his dad, would go into the trust. Seth and his parents were to go through Mr. Garber's personal possessions—everything in the house and the garage. They could keep what they wanted and sell what they didn't want, with the proceeds to be put into a bank account in the name of the trust. Garber's house was to be rented out and the income from the rental would go into the trust. Mr. Banks would be paid a modest annual fee for trust maintenance.

When Seth turned eighteen, he could decide what to do with Garber's house and grounds, which included several acres of timberland on the slope leading down to the old log pond. He could assume ownership or direct Mr. Banks to sell the property and turn the proceeds over to him.

"That about covers it," the attorney said. "Any questions or concerns? Anything you'd like to have changed?"

Seth didn't know enough about finances or legal matters to have questions or concerns. He'd been included in the meeting, but he was certain no one really cared about his opinion. So he was surprised when his dad said, "What do you think, son? Does all that sound okay to you?"

Seth thought for a moment, quickly concluding

that his mother had the right idea in deferring to his dad in the matter. "If it sounds okay to you, Dad, then it's okay with me. You would know what's best."

"My only concern," his dad said to Mr. Banks, "is that managing rental property can be a headache."

"That is a consideration," the attorney said, "but I have a suggestion that might ease your concern. I have a few rentals myself. They're managed by an agency that takes care of everything for a percentage of the monthly rent. They screen applicants, collect the rent, hire maintenance workers as needed, things like that. They've done a good job for me. We can use them for this property if you'd like."

"That would be fine," Seth's dad said. "I think holding on to the property for now and generating some income makes sense. But I'm wondering if a portion of that income could be channeled into one of those college savings accounts for Seth."

"Excellent idea," the attorney said. "I'll have that added to the final draft." He paused, glancing in turn at Seth and his dad. "If we're all in agreement, then, I'll have the papers drawn up for signatures. As for renting out the house, the sooner the better. It isn't good to leave a country home vacant for long. Squatters can take over, and that's a headache you definitely don't want."

"Very well," Seth's dad said. "We'll begin going through Mr. Garber's belongings as soon as we can. I should have some free time this weekend. That all right with you, Seth?"

That was more than all right with Seth. Ever since

he'd found out about his inheritance, he'd been eager to get back into Mr. Garber's house and go through his stuff. There had to be something there that would reveal more about his mysterious benefactor.

"Can Collin come with us?"

"I don't see why not," his dad said. "At least this time you boys won't be breaking the law."

25

ON SATURDAY MORNING, Seth and his dad picked up Collin in the truck they used for hauling firewood. "Thanks for letting me come along, Mr. Roberson," Collin said.

Seth's dad laughed. "You might not be thanking me after you see how much work there is to be done."

But, as usual, Collin's sense of adventure was not to be deterred. "This is gonna be fun," he said, his enthusiasm bubbling up like soda fizz. He poked Seth in the ribs with his elbow. "Like going on a treasure hunt, right?"

"Right," Seth said, not wanting to dampen his friend's fervor. He was excited too, but in a different way. For him, going through Mr. Garber's things wasn't so much a treasure hunt as it was an excavation of the man's life.

Seth's dad turned onto Fir Hill Road, followed its winding uphill path to where it ended, and headed up the gravel drive to Garber's property. He parked in the shade in front of the house. Although the pine-scented air still carried the fresh breath of morning, the day promised to be a scorcher.

Seth glimpsed the yellow sheriff's tape that still encircled the house. It had sagged and spiraled and, in places, drooped nearly to the ground. At the front door, Seth's dad tore an opening in the tape and tossed the ends aside. He opened the door with the key Mr. Banks had given him, and the boys followed him inside.

They were greeted by a tsunami of warm, stale air. "Boys," Seth's dad said, "I think the first order of business is to open all the windows and get some fresh air flowing through this place. You two do that while I look around and take stock of what we're dealing with here."

The boys went through the house opening windows. Seth opened the one in the furnished bedroom and found the bottom of its screen pushed out. He pulled it in and snapped it back in place.

"That's all of them," Collin said as he emerged from the bedroom with the sleeping bag and the blacked-out window.

When they rejoined Seth's dad, he was standing in the living room with his hands on his hips and a dubious look on his face. "It's going to take a lot of work to make this place rentable. We've got to clear out all of Mr. Garber's stuff, and then the house will need some serious cleaning." He tucked in an errant shirttail. "I think the thing to do is to hire a cleaning crew to come in and give it a good going-over."

Seth thought that was a good idea. He saw nothing adventuresome about "serious cleaning."

"That leaves us with the task of sorting through

everything in the house and deciding what to do with it all," his dad said.

"What about the stuff in the garage?" Seth asked.

"We'll leave that for later."

"Where do you want to start, Mr. Roberson?" Collin asked, ready for action.

Seth's dad gazed around pensively. "The kitchen will probably take the longest," he said, "so let's start there. Here's what I have in mind: Whatever we find that's salvageable—that is, potentially useful to someone—we'll box up and take to Goodwill. The unsalvageable stuff—the stuff that even Goodwill wouldn't want—we'll bag and haul off to the dump, along with most of this old furniture, which has definitely seen its day. When we come across something we think is worth keeping, we'll set it aside and take it home. How does that sound?"

"Fine," Seth said.

"More than fine," said Collin, obviously ready to get on with the treasure hunt.

They brought in cardboard boxes and heavy-duty trash bags from the truck. In the kitchen, Collin emptied out the refrigerator while Seth assisted his dad in going through all the drawers and cabinets. When finished there, they moved on to the other rooms of the house.

In a hall closet, Seth found a tattered doggy tug toy in the form of an end-knotted length of rope. He sighed as he recalled his failed attempt to reclaim Henry Garber's dog. It was the day after he'd learned of his inheritance. Without telling his parents, he had called Saving Grace Pet Adoption Center, the local animal shelter, and inquired about the dog.

He explained to the lady who answered the phone what dog he was talking about, giving her a description, the date it had been brought to the shelter and by whom (animal control), and the name of the owner (now deceased). Seth didn't claim that the dog belonged to him, only that his family was interested in adopting it. The lady put him on hold while she checked the shelter's records.

"I'm sorry," she said, "that dog has been adopted out. But if you go to our website, you'll see photos and descriptions of our other wonderful pets that need a good home."

Seth's voice was thick in his throat when he thanked her and hung up. It was nice that the dog had been adopted by someone. Still, it seemed only right that he should have been the new owner.

"Pond Dog," he muttered as he stuffed the tug toy into a trash bag, "you won't be happy anywhere else."

It took well into the afternoon, with a break to eat a picnic lunch Seth's mom had sent, to go through everything in the house and get it boxed or bagged. As it turned out, they found very little worth keeping.

To Collin's dismay, they discovered no hidden treasures among Mr. Garber's belongings: no valuable coin collection, no gold-plated belt buckle, no antique pocket watch, no diamond-studded tie clip, no hundred-dollar bills stuffed in socks or sewn into the lining of clothing. But more disappointing to Seth, they'd come across no personal items that would have told him more about Mr. Garber and his past.

175

Collin had set aside one item: the old man's bayonet. "I'll take it if you don't want it," he told Seth.

"You can have it," Seth said.

"What about you, son?" Seth's dad asked as they stood amid the jumble of stuffed bags and packed boxes in the living room. "Anything you want?"

Seth hesitated, unsure his dad would approve. "I'd like to take the little desk," he said, walking over to it, "and the stuff in it. If that's okay." He'd already reinserted the desk's drawer and replaced its contents that had spilled out onto the floor. "I think I can find space for it in my room."

"That's fine, son," his dad said. "I'll help you refinish it, if you'd like."

"Thanks, Dad—I'd like that."

"And I found something else you might want to keep," his dad said. He withdrew an unusual-looking pair of binoculars from one of the boxes and handed them to Seth. They were bulky and had an olive-green casing. "They're military grade. High-powered. Expensive, I would imagine."

Seth held them up to his eyes, but all he saw was a blur. He pulled them away, feeling a little dizzy. "I know right where I'll keep them," he said. He opened the desk drawer and placed them inside.

They loaded all the Goodwill boxes into the truck, along with the desk. Seth's dad slammed the tailgate shut, his face glistening with sweat. "I'll have to make a run to the dump to haul off all the trash bags and the unwanted furniture." He took an openmouthed breath, his cheeks puffing when he blew it out. "Another day. But before we go, we'd better close and lock all the windows. We don't want to

176

make it easy for squatters."

The boys went around closing and locking windows. Seth slid the one in Garber's bedroom shut. As he was leaving the room, he glanced into the clothes closet. *Oh, we forgot the hats.* They had cleared the closet of its hanging clothes but hadn't taken the hats sitting on the shelf above them.

The shelf held an assortment of hats: an angler bucket hat, a broad-brimmed straw hat, an Indiana Jones hat, a cowboy hat, a rain hat, a stocking cap, and several baseball caps. Mr. Garber, Seth recalled, always wore a hat when he came down to the pond to fish.

One of the baseball caps caught Seth's attention. Embroidered on its front panel was the image of a dog—possibly a Saint Bernard—and below that the logo BIG DOGS. He had never seen Mr. Garber wear that hat.

"You get lost?"

It was Collin, standing behind him.

"We forgot the hats," Seth said, peering up at the shelf.

"Leave 'em for now," Collin said.

Seth pointed at the cap with the dog on it. "I want that one." He leaped up and grabbed for the cap but fell short.

Collin laughed. "Okay—move aside." He flexed his knees, sprang into the air, and snatched the cap off the shelf.

When he did, a small metal box tumbled down and crashed to the floor at Seth's feet. He jumped back. "Oh!"

"What going on?" Seth's dad said, entering the

room. He saw the box and picked it up. "What's this?"

Collin showed him the BIG DOGS cap. "I pulled this off the shelf and the box came down with it."

"It must have been under the cap," Seth said.

His dad studied the box. Its lid had remained closed in the fall. "Looks like an old cash box."

Collin's eyes sparkled. "Maybe it's full of rubies and diamonds."

Seth's dad shook the box. It didn't rattle.

"Probably just hundred dollar bills," Seth said in jest.

"Might need a key to open it," his dad said, indicating a key slot in the latch mechanism. But when he pressed the latch button, the lid popped open.

"Hmm," he said, thumbing through the box's contents. "Photographs—and from the looks of them, very old ones." He took one out and examined it. "Sailor boys. Probably some of Mr. Garber's buddies from Vietnam." He showed the photo to the boys.

Seth felt a surge of excitement. "Is Mr. Garber in the picture?"

His dad squinted. "Hard to tell. They're all so young looking. Hardly out of their teens, I'd guess." He turned the photograph over. "No names."

"I heard that boys fifteen or sixteen lied about their age so they could go to war," Collin said.

"Maybe during the world wars," Seth's dad said. "Not so much when it came to Vietnam. Not many boys—or men—were eager to go fight in the jungles over there. As a matter of fact, a lot of young men skipped off to Canada to avoid being drafted."

"Drafted?" Collin said. "You mean like the pro football teams do with college players?"

Seth's dad chuckled uneasily. "Something like that. Except the military draft was one you didn't want to get selected for."

"Because they'd send you off to a foreign country to kill people?"

"A sad reality—yes," Seth's dad said. "Although, if I'd had to fight in a war and someone shot at me, I guess I'd have shot back too."

He shuffled through the other photos, taking out a few more. The boys craned their necks to see. The pictures were all similar: uniformed sailors in pairs or small groups in various poses, sometimes looking deadly serious, sometimes mugging for the camera.

Seth's dad rifled to the bottom of the box and brought out a photograph printed on different paper than the others. As he looked at it, his eyes wandered for a moment before resettling on the picture. He dropped it back into the box without showing it to the boys and closed the lid.

"More sailors?" Seth asked.

His dad tucked the box under his arm. "We'd better head out now, boys. I want to get to Goodwill before it closes." He started for the front door with the boys at his heels.

Seth felt something land on his head. He reached up and pulled it off. It was the cap with the dog logo on it.

"Don't want to forget your dog," Collin said.

"Right," Seth said, smiling as he snugged the cap down on his head, almost covering his eyes.

26

SETH THOUGHT THAT HIS MOTHER might push back
on his desire to keep Mr. Garber's desk and put it in
his room, but she didn't.

"Actually, son," his dad told him, "I think you
picked the one thing your mother didn't mind your
bringing home."

"Why is that?"

"Because her grandparents had a similar desk in
their parlor. It was where your Great-grandmother
Nelly sat and wrote letters; she was a dedicated letter writer. If I recall correctly, your mother's older
sister, your Aunt Sheila, who lives back east now,
inherited the desk." He lowered his voice. "I don't
think your mother was any too happy about that,
because she'd had her eye on the desk as well."

Seth chuckled. "Well then I guess it's a good thing
I kept the desk and let Collin have the bayonet?"

"A very good thing."

One day not long after that, they got a surprise
visit from Deputy Waller, who brought Seth something else of Mr. Garber's: his fishing rod and reel

and tackle box.

"These were in his boat when we found it," the deputy said. "We kept them as potential evidence, but with the case closed and the way things turned out, I thought you might want to have them."

"Yessir, I would," Seth said. "Thank you." He didn't know what he was going to do with the fishing gear. He'd never seen the fun in drowning worms or mindlessly casting lures. But keeping it seemed like the thing to do, since seeing Mr. Garber out on the pond fishing was the thing he remembered most about the man.

A few weeks later, Seth went with his dad back to Garber's house. His dad wanted to check on the work that had been done on the place. After the cleaning crew had completed their work, Seth's dad had decided that cleaning wasn't enough, so he'd hired a contractor to paint the inside of the house and scrape the black paint off the windowpanes in the second bedroom.

"It's not a castle," Seth's dad said as he and Seth walked through the house. "But at least it doesn't stink anymore."

Seth thought it stunk of new paint.

During the time the house was being worked on, Seth and Collin sometimes went up to Garber's place just for fun, making sure to stay out of the way of the workers. They roamed the grounds, imagining themselves barons of a great country estate. They combed the woods for signs of Bigfoot. They scouted for the perfect location for a tree house—the higher up the better, according to Collin. On occasion, they would come across a paper wasp nest hanging balloon-like from a tree branch. When that happened, they would knock it down with a stick and then try to outrun the angry swarm. Getting stung a few times was a sign of valor.

On one such day, after a morning's romp around the grounds, the boys climbed up on top of the big round woodpile next to Garber's house, because it seemed like the thing to do.

"You know what would be great?" Collin said as he peered through a break in the trees at the valley below.

"What?"

"A zip line."

"Zip line?" Seth had never seen an actual zip line. He'd only seen them on TV. But he knew that Collin had ridden one in Colorado when he went there once with his parents to visit his brother, who'd been in a car accident and was in the hospital.

"This would be a perfect place for one," Collin said. "From here you could zip all the way down to the bottom of the hill and almost end up in the pond. And look," he said, pointing, "you can see your house from here."

Seth sat up taller and stretched his neck. It was true. It was a long-range view, but there it was—the front of his house, the steps leading up to the porch, the porch swing.

"Just think," Collin said, "you could zip down the hill and be home in two minutes."

Seth laughed. "You get the craziest ideas."

"It's not crazy. It's practical."

"Well, then, it's practically crazy."

Collin made a goofy, cross-eyed face. "I don't even know what that means."

"I don't either," Seth said and laughed. Then Collin laughed too, and seeing him laugh made Seth laugh harder. Before long, they were both shaking with laughter. And the harder they laughed, the more they shook. They shook so much that they dislodged some logs from the firewood stack they were sitting on.

"Whoa," Seth said, feeling movement beneath him. He glanced at Collin, whose round eyes told him that he'd felt it too.

"I think we'd—" Collin said. But before he could get out any more words, the pile of firewood beneath them imploded like a volcanic cone collapsing. A terrifying instant later, the boys found themselves buried in a mesh of split logs.

"Are you okay?" Collin said, pushing wood aside.

"I think so," Seth said, though he wasn't sure. "I'm gonna have some sore ribs, I know that."

Collin got up and waded through firewood to where Seth lay. "That was crazy." He grinned. "Practically crazy anyway."

"Don't make me laugh," Seth said as he struggled to sit up. "It hurts to laugh."

"Now you tell me."

Not long after that, Seth found out that Mr. Garber's house had been rented to a young couple who'd recently had a baby. Their names were Randy and Sara Young. They'd moved to the area from Texas because Randy had gotten a job at a local boat manufacturing company.

"Now I know that technically that house belongs

to you, Seth—or it will someday," his mother told him. "But I don't want you and Collin going up there anymore and bothering that young couple."

"That's not fair," Collin said when Seth broke the news to him. "It's your house."

Seth didn't think it was fair either. But he wasn't about to say that to his mother because he knew what she would say. She'd say what she always said whenever he complained about the unfairness of something: "Fairness has nothing to do with it. What's right isn't always fair. And the sooner you learn that, the better." It wasn't an easy lesson to learn.

27

AS IT DID EACH SUMMER, the log pond receded
from its banks. The hot afternoon breezes blow-dried
its surface, and the absence of rain hastened its retreat. By mid-August, the pond's broad banks were
cracked and crusted like sunburned lips.

The pond changed in other ways as well. The cat-
tails in the shallows turned brown and set free their
fluffy seeds to ride gossamer-like on the warm air.
Submerged branches broke through the surface,
looking like scarecrow limbs. A rise in water temperature, along with a buildup of nutrients, caused an
algae bloom that painted the water along the shore
neon green. Patches of scum floated on the surface,
giving off an unpleasant, musty odor.

The boys might have avoided the pond this time of
year except for one thing: the wild blackberries were
at their peak of ripeness. They hung in tantalizing
clusters from the thickets of vines that ringed the
pond.

As he always did during the first ten minutes of picking, Seth ate as many blackberries as he dropped into the container hanging from his belt. His dad had shown him how to make it. You cut an opening in the top of a one-gallon plastic water jug, slip your belt through the handle loop, and cinch the belt tightly around your waist. That leaves both hands free for picking and, when the urge strikes, for popping the juicy berries into your mouth.

Not surprisingly, Collin was the faster picker. That was because Seth scrupulously avoided the wicked thorns on the berry vines, whereas Collin eagerly reached into tangles of creepers to pluck plump berries that were out of Seth's safe reach. At the end of every picking session, Collin's forearms were crosshatched with scratches, some oozing blood. He considered it a badge of honor.

"Mom wants two quarts today," Collin said as he cheerfully went about his work. "One for a pie and one for a cobbler."

"My mom's making jam," Seth said.

There were plenty of berries to harvest. Even in the waning days of summer, when the native grasses withered and crunched underfoot, leaves on the oak trees curled for lack of moisture, and you needed a pickaxe to dig a hole in the ground, the wild blackberry bushes flourished.

"I can't believe we have to go back to school in a few weeks," Collin said.

Seth licked blackberry juice from his fingers before going back to picking. "Yeah, not a happy thought—especially this year."

The school year traditionally began the day after

Labor Day, and this year was no exception. What was different was that Seth and Collin would be transitioning from elementary school to middle school.

"You think they'll really pile on the homework?" Collin said.

"I'm not worried about homework. I just don't want some eighth grader giving me a swirly."

It was rumored at the elementary schools that some of the eighth-grade boys at the middle school would choose a sixth grader they didn't like, stick his head in a toilet, and then flush it.

"They better not try that with me," Collin said. "I'll flatten the first one who does."

But Seth couldn't see himself "flattening" anybody, much less an eighth grader. He'd just have to stay out of their way.

"My jug's full," Collin said, "and I'm thirsty. Let's scoot."

Seth checked his jug. "I'm not done, and I don't want to have to come back. It's hot and it's only gonna get hotter."

"Let's get you filled up, then," Collin said and began dropping all the berries he picked into Seth's container. Soon it was brimming with berries.

The boys parted company then with plans to meet at Collin's house later.

When he got home with his bounty of berries, Seth was glad to see his grandmother's car parked in the driveway. She hadn't come around in a few weeks, and whenever he'd asked his mom about it, all she would say was, "Grandma's not been feeling well these days."

Seth gathered that his dad hadn't been feeling well these days either. He'd been quieter than usual at the dinner table, and evenings he would take the newspaper into the den and close the door, a sign for the kids to stay out.

Entering the kitchen, Seth found Grandma Claire seated at the breakfast nook, her hands cradling a coffee cup. His mom sat beside her. His dad was there too, sitting on the bench seat across from them. It was Friday afternoon and his dad should have been at work. He must have taken the afternoon off, something he occasionally did.

Seth set the container of blackberries on the counter. "A full jug like you wanted, Mom," he said proudly. "Hi, Grandma." He went over and gave her a hug. "I'm glad you're feeling better." She returned his hug, clinging to him longer than usual.

He got a glass from a cupboard and filled it with cold water from the refrigerator. He guzzled half of it. "Can I go over to Collin's now? It's super hot outside. Collin said it was okay with his mom if we played video games at his house."

His dad answered. "Maybe later, son. For now, we'd like you to sit with us. Your grandmother has something to tell you."

Seth's first thought was, *What did I do wrong, and why is Grandma Claire delivering the news?* What he said was, "Where's Baylie?"

"At the Caseys'," his mother said. "Brownie meeting."

"Oh." He drank the rest of the water and sat down beside his dad. "So, Grandma, what did you want to tell me?"

Grandma Claire took a sip from her cup and smiled dolefully. "Let me show you something first," she said, her voice raspier than normal. In front of her on the table was a brown envelope. She opened it, pulled out a photograph, and slid it across to him.

Curious, Seth picked it up and looked at it. It was a black-and-white photo, an old one from the looks of it, crinkled and frayed around the edges. It was a picture of a young man in a sailor's uniform, sitting on a porch swing beside a young woman who was leaning against him with her head on his shoulder.

"Who's this?" he asked.

His dad said, "It's one of the photographs from the metal box we found in Mr. Garber's closet."

"The pictures of the sailor boys," Seth said. He remembered the photos, but not this one. "Who are these people? Do you know, Grandma?"

She nodded solemnly. "I do." She reached into the envelope again, withdrew another photo, and handed it to him.

Seth stared at it, confused. He placed it on the table alongside the first one. The two photographs looked just alike, except that the second one was in better condition. "They're the same picture," he said. He tapped the edge of the second one. "Where did this one come from?"

Grandma Claire took a deep breath and let it out slowly. "It's been in a box tucked away in my closet for the last forty-something years."

Forty years? Seth picked up the two photographs and examined them again, his eyes going back and forth between them. He studied the faces of the young couple in the one photo, then in the other.

189

The photographs were indeed identical.

"I don't understand," he said, shaking his head. "Who *are* these people?"

He looked across the table at his grandmother. Tears flooded from her eyes.

28

SETH'S GRANDMOTHER DABBED at her tears with a wadded tissue. "I want to tell you a story," she said to Seth, a look of desolation in her eyes. "It's the story of me and Henry Thomas Garber."

Grandma Claire and Henry Garber? Seth held up the two photos. "Is this you and . . .?" *How could it be?*

"Yes," his grandmother said. "And I owe you an explanation."

An explanation? What explanation could possibly account for what she was saying? What was he missing here? He looked to his dad for a clue.

"Just listen to your grandmother, son, and then we'll talk."

Grandma Claire met Seth's baffled gaze. "When I was eighteen years old," she said, "I was still living at home with my parents in New Jersey, in a suburb of Trenton. I had graduated from high school and was working as a sales clerk at J.C. Penney. One Saturday night I was out at a pizza parlor with friends, and they introduced me to a young man named Henry. He was twenty years old. He worked in high-rise construction, he said. He was handsome, I thought, but very self-contained. You know, the strong, silent type—and that appealed to me at the time.

"I saw him again later at a party, and another time at a city league softball game a few guys I knew played in. What I didn't know was that our mutual friends had been prompting him to ask me out on a date. Finally, one night he did."

She took a sip from her cup. "We started dating and soon fell in love. Six months later, against the advice of my parents, who thought we were rushing things—and we were—we got married. It was a small wedding with a few friends and family, all on my side.

"Henry didn't have any family in the area. He was from the Upper Peninsula of Michigan and had left home soon after graduating from high school. His father had died when Henry was young, and his mother had remarried. Henry had an older brother and an older sister, but they had already left home by then. He and his stepfather didn't get along. Henry didn't talk much about it. But it was obvious from what little he did say that it was a bitter relationship that strained his mother's marriage. That's why he left home when he did, and why he'd had little contact with family since leaving. I don't think they even knew he'd gotten married."

Seth's thoughts swirled dizzyingly as he tried to make sense of what his grandmother was saying. She and Henry Garber, married and living in New Jersey? It was so far-fetched.

"Not long after our wedding," she went on, "Henry lost his job. The contractor he was working for was arrested for bribing city officials to get favorable treatment on building contracts. Henry had a hard time finding another job. It was as if he and his co-workers were being punished for what their boss had allegedly done.

"I still had my job at Penney's, but with Henry not working, we struggled financially. That really bothered him, and the longer the situation lasted, the more frustrated he became. One day, without any discussion, he informed me that he was going to join the military. His dad had been a Seabee—a member of the United States Naval Construction Battalion—and Henry decided to follow in his footsteps.

"I was opposed to the idea. The Vietnam War was still going on, and the thought of Henry going off to fight terrified me. But he had made up his mind. I needn't worry, he said, the war was winding down and would probably be over before he was done with his training."

Grandma Claire scoffed. "He was wrong about that. He went through eight weeks of navy boot camp and then ten weeks of Seabee training. A week later, he was shipped off to Vietnam. The photo you have there, Seth, was taken the morning of the day he left. Later, when I had the film developed, I had an extra copy made and sent it to him."

She closed her eyes briefly as if to steel herself for what came next. "I'll never forget that day. I cried so hard I thought I would die. I couldn't eat, couldn't sleep, couldn't work. I was convinced I'd never see my beloved Henry again. My mother, who was very religious, gave him a medallion to carry, one with the image of some saint on it. She said it would keep him safe. She even had his initials engraved on the back of it."

She laughed derisively. "So much for the Seabees. When Henry got to Vietnam, instead of assigning him to a construction battalion, the Navy dispatched him to a river patrol unit. Their job was to travel the rivers and look for infiltrators from the north and traffickers in weapons and ammunition. They patrolled day and night. Henry wrote me letters and told me some of what happened on the river, but he deliberately left out anything that would make me worry about his safety.

"Well," Seth's grandmother said with a heavy sigh, "about two months after Henry left for Vietnam, I found out I was pregnant. I didn't know what to do. I knew I should write and tell him, but I was afraid it would only distract him from his duties, so I put it off. My mother felt strongly that I should let him know, and the sooner the better. She said that even if something happened to him, he'd want to know he had fathered a child. I was almost five months along when I finally gave him the news in a letter.

"It was quite some time before I heard back from him. Getting mail in and out of the war zone was difficult at times. His response shocked me. He said, 'Is the baby mine?' How could he ask such a question? I wrote him back and assured him the baby was his, but I don't know if he really believed me."

She swallowed hard and continued, her voice getting weaker the longer she spoke. "Henry's tour of duty in Vietnam was supposed to be eleven months.

But it got extended three months, and then another three months. It was almost eighteen months before he got home. By then we had a toddler. Little David," she said with a fleeting smile.

David? Seth looked at his dad.

His dad nodded. "That's right, son. Henry Garber was my biological father."

Seth could hardly believe what he was hearing. "But, Dad, why—"

"Please, son, let your grandmother finish."

"So," she said, picking up again, "my worst fear— that Henry would be killed in the war—was never realized. But there was another consequence of war I hadn't counted on: PTSD."

The mention of PTSD set off an explosion of thoughts in Seth's head. "Post-traumatic stress disorder—I know what that is, and it's bad. Mr. Winkelman told me about it, and I read more about it online."

"So I heard," his grandmother said. "And you're right. It's worse than you can ever imagine."

She paused, a distant look in her eyes. "When Henry came back from the war, he wasn't himself. He tried to adjust to life back home, but it was a terrible struggle for him. Whatever he'd gone through in the war stuck in his head and he couldn't get it out. He had difficulty sleeping, and when he did sleep, he had nightmares that woke him.

"Because he wasn't sleeping well, he became irritable. Any little annoyance set him off. He'd get angry, and sometimes the anger triggered outbursts that frightened me. When I tried to calm him down, he would get in my face and yell at me, saying I didn't understand what he was going through. He was right—I didn't. And then he would storm out of the house and sometimes be gone for days. When he came home, he remained silent and emotionally distant.

"I worried about him. I knew he was depressed, and his depression only caused him to withdraw further into himself. He knew he had a problem, but he refused to talk to me or anyone else about it. 'Talking about it doesn't help,' he insisted.

"I begged him to go see the doctors at the VA, and finally he did. They gave him medicine for anxiety and depression, but it was of little help."

She shook her head mournfully, as if remembering grieved her. "During this time, he was assigned to a naval ammunition depot within commuting distance of an apartment we had rented west of Trenton. When he started having problems at work, everything came to a head, because his military bosses weren't as understanding as I was. He was disciplined for various infractions—being late for work, not showing up at all, not following orders. One day, he got into an argument with a fellow seaman and punched him in the face. He was locked up in the stockade for three days.

"Things at work only got worse after that, and eventually he was given a medical discharge from the navy. That's when the bottom fell out for him. His symptoms—the depression, the irritability, the angry outbursts—all but consumed him. In his nightmares he relived episodes of combat. He would wake up in the middle of the night screaming and thrashing around in bed like a wild man. It was awful—just *awful.*"

The tears were back in Grandma Claire's eyes. "That was the beginning of the end for us—for our marriage," she said, her lips trembling. "There were times when I was so afraid to be around him that I took little David and stayed with my parents. Henry didn't blame me. He knew that when his attacks came on, he was not only a danger to himself but also to me and the baby.

"Finally, afraid he'd harm me or David, Henry begged me to divorce him. 'I love you,' he said, 'and I'll always love you, but for your safety and happiness—and the baby's—you must get as far away from me as you can. And don't tell me where you are.'

"I told him I wouldn't do it, that I couldn't just abandon him. I wanted to help him get better! But he insisted, and my parents pleaded with me to do as he asked. They said it was best for everyone, and that what Henry was asking proved how much he loved me."

She wiped her eyes with the tissue. "I didn't know what else to do, so in the end, I agreed. I filed for divorce and went back to using my maiden name, Ellsworth. I had a cousin who lived in Bend, so little David and I came out to Oregon. We lived with my cousin's family until I was able to get a job and an apartment of my own. The man I worked for had a son named Harold. Over time, Harold and I grew close."

Seth blinked hard as he tried to make room in his head for another surprising revelation. "Grandpa Hal?"

"One and the same," his grandmother said. "In due course, Harold and I married. We moved to the Roseburg area not long after that when he took a job with the Douglas County Building Department."

She took a snuffling breath. "By then, three years had passed since I'd left New Jersey with David and come west. During that time, and for the next five years, I never heard from or anything about Henry Garber.

"Then one day, like a ghost from the past, he showed up on my doorstep. Thankfully, your dad was in school and Harold at work. I was stunned to say the least. I stood there speechless, thinking I must be hallucinating.

"Henry was curiously calm. He was neatly dressed and well groomed. And though the passing of years showed in his face—his lips had thinned and his eyes had wrinkles at their corners—he was still handsome in a weather-beaten way.

"He asked if he could come inside and talk to me. I was scared and confused and didn't know what to do. I'd loved him once but had since moved on. I had a new life with Harold and was happy. He promised to stay only a few minutes. Dazed and confused, I let him in.

"We sat in the living room. I was trembling all over and my heart was pounding dreadfully. All I could think of was how my happy new life was about to be shattered by this phantom from my past.

"I asked him why he was there, what he wanted, and how he had found me.

"He said in a restrained, sincere voice that the first few years after we divorced were hell for him. He drank a lot, got into drugs. He lived on the streets for a while. Got arrested a few times. Served time in jail for breaking and entering. Through an inmate drug diversion program, he eventually got sober and straightened out his life.

"He said that he'd been off drugs for the last five years and, with the help of counseling and medication, had managed to get his PTSD under control. He said, 'I waited five years to make sure I was okay—okay being relative—before trying to find you.'

"I asked what he meant by that. He said that he knew he would never be *totally* okay, that he'd always have to be on guard against episodes of PTSD, but that he knew the signs now and knew how to cope. He had found me by going through my parents' trash and finding an envelope with my return address on it.

"I asked him again why he was there and what he wanted from me.

"I needn't worry, he told me. He wasn't there to cause problems for me or my family. 'All I want,' he said, 'is to watch my son grow up.'"

Grandma Claire's mouth fell open, as it must have all those years ago when Henry Garber spoke those words to her. "I was stupefied," she said. "It was an outrageous request, and he made it sound as if it was no big deal. 'And how do you intend to do that?' I asked. His answer shook me to the core.

"He said that he'd bought the old house on the hill above the pond. He was going to move in and live there.

"I was beside myself. 'You can't do that!' I cried. 'That's an invasion of our privacy!' We could see that house from our front porch, which meant that he could see our house from there. 'We'll move,' I told him.

"'I found you once,' he said, 'and I can find you again.'

"'Please don't do this,' I begged him. 'Please, don't.' I was crying uncontrollably by then.

"Henry was quiet for a time. Then he looked at me with a longing that could only have come from the depths of one's soul. 'Claire,' he said, 'please allow me this one thing. I have nothing else to live for. And I promise you, I will never again contact you. Nor will I ever contact your husband, or David. I'll be the ghost who lives in the house on the hill. And your silence is all I ask.'"

Seth's grandmother gazed across the table at him, her eyes pleading for understanding. "I didn't know what to say. I hated the thought of it. But what could I do? I knew I couldn't stop him. So, as unwilling as I was to accept what he was asking of me, I felt I had no choice."

She shuddered. "I was a nervous wreck for a while after that, even as I did my best to go on as if nothing had changed. Harold knew something was wrong, but I convinced him that I was just concerned about my mother's health, which was failing.

"And Henry was true to his word. He kept to himself. He never called me or came to see me again, or made contact with your dad or Harold. I knew he was up there on the hill, watching, but I tried not to think about it. I tried to pretend that his visit hadn't been real, only a dream.

"Weeks and months went by without further contact with Henry, and I began to relax. It became easier and easier for me to put him out of my mind. Your dad grew up blissfully ignorant, accepting Harold as the loving father he was."

She smiled feebly. "Then years flew by, and your dad and mom got married, and you were born and then Baylie. By then, I'd all but forgotten about Henry Garber, or had convinced myself that he didn't really exist."

The smile vanished. "But when you and Collin started mentioning the old man who came down to the pond to fish, I knew it had to be Henry. But I dared not say anything, other than to admonish you boys to keep your distance from him."

A note of despair seeped into her voice. "Even when he drowned—and how awful that you and Collin had to be the ones to find the body—I couldn't bring myself to tell anyone that I knew who he was and why they couldn't find any next of kin."

She pressed her hands to her chest. "And that day at his memorial service . . ."

She broke down then. Her face contorted and her tears flowed in torrents. "Seth, dear Seth," she said through desperate gasps, "I'm so sorry to have kept all of this from you until now. You're the one who cared about Henry when no one else did. You're the one who made it happen that he was given a proper burial with military honors, finally receiving the recognition for his service to our country that he deserved. It was you . . . all you."

She buried her face in her hands and continued to sob. "I'm so sorry . . . about everything."

29

SETH AND HIS DAD were in the living room. His dad was tilted back in his recliner. Seth, feeling emotionally unraveled, sat on the floor propped up against the sofa.

Grandma Claire had gone home. Seth's mother had gone to stay with her, and she was to pick up Baylie on her way. "She shouldn't be alone tonight," his mother had told his dad, who'd agreed.

Seth was still trying to wrap his mind around his grandmother's account of her relationship with Henry Garber. She had opened the door to her past, exposing herself to the painful memories that came rushing out. He had witnessed her anguish and felt sorry for her. But he was also shaken—her narrative was an assault on the world as he had come to know it. He was being asked to accept a new reality that included Mr. Garber as a long-lost member of his family—his own grandfather!—and that was mind-boggling.

"Dad," he said, "when we were going through the box of photos at Mr. Garber's house and you saw the one of the young couple on the porch swing, did you know right away that it was Grandma in the picture with him?"

"No," his dad said, "I didn't know who the people in the picture were. They were both so young, and people's looks change a lot as they age. I only knew that I'd seen the photograph somewhere before, and I thought I knew where."

"In Grandma's stuff?"

His dad adjusted his chair to an upright position. "Exactly. You see, when your grandpa Harold died, we wanted a photograph of him to appear in the newspaper with his obituary. Sometimes with obituaries, two photos are used—a more current one of the deceased and one taken when they were younger. Your grandma thought that would be a good thing to do for Hal's obit.

"We found a recent one of him that your grandma liked, but we didn't have one of him when he was younger. She told me that we might find one in a box of old photos she kept in a closet. She didn't feel like going through them herself, so your mother and I offered to do it. We found a nice picture of your grandpa taken about the time he and your grandmother got married, and she gave us the okay to use it.

"But while going through the photos, we came across the one with the young sailor and the girl sitting on the porch swing. I didn't know who they were or where the picture had been taken. Nothing in the photo looked familiar. I'd meant to ask your grandmother about it, but with everything going on at the time, planning your grandfather's funeral and all, I never got around to it. As time went by, I forgot about the picture. But then that day at Mr. Garber's house, when we were going through his photographs and I saw the same picture, it jogged my memory."

"And you asked Grandma about it?"

Seth's dad shook his head. "Not right away. I showed the photo to your mother. She didn't recall having seen it before. But she was of the opinion that the woman in the picture was your grandmother. 'Look at the high cheekbones,' she said, 'and the full lips.'

"I wasn't so sure. Also, I'd had only the one brief contact with Mr. Garber, and that when he was much older. So I didn't recognize him either."

His brow pinched. "But the more I thought about it, the more I became convinced that the young woman in the picture was my mother and the sailor Henry Garber. Why else would he have a copy of the same photograph she had? This meant that your grandmother must have known Garber, and had known him for a long time. But I was still confused and unsure of what to do. If it was true that she'd had a relationship with Henry Garber, why hadn't she come right out and said so, instead of hiding the fact?

"Ultimately, I decided that it was a question that needed to be answered, so I resolved to talk to her about it. One day after work, I dropped by her apartment and showed her the photograph. I told her where it had come from."

Seth sat up straighter. "What did she say?"

"She didn't say anything for some time—just sat staring at the picture, tears welling up in her eyes.

Finally, she admitted that it was her and Henry Garber sitting on that porch swing. Then after she stopped crying, which took a while, she told me the same story she just told you."

Seth imagined that it must have been a terrible scene, Grandma Claire pouring her heart out to his dad while he tried to cope with the reality-shattering impact of it all. He wondered how his dad had felt at that moment, and he asked him about it.

His dad heaved a sigh. "I was angry at first that she'd waited so long to tell me. But mostly I was sad. Sad for your grandmother, sad for Henry Garber, and, yes, maybe a bit sad for myself that I'd never had the chance to get to know my biological father. But they both had their reasons for not wanting me to know, and I think they were valid reasons. They kept their secret out of love and caring for me—and for you. And, of course, your grandmother didn't want to hurt your grandfather Harold. And I think his finding out would have been terribly hard on him."

"So you think she did the right thing by not telling us?" Seth asked.

His dad smiled sympathetically. "I think she did what she thought was right. And that's all you can ask of a person."

"So you're not mad at Grandma anymore?"

"No, I'm not mad at her. She's been through quite enough. It must have been a heavy burden for her to bear, having to keep such a secret all these years."

Seth was of the same mind. And it pleased him to know that his dad harbored no resentment toward Grandma Claire, because it helped him sort out his own feelings. "Then I'm not mad at her either," he said. "Although it would have been nice to know some of this stuff sooner, because it does kind of explain why Mr. Garber left all his property to me." *Kind of—but not totally.* "But why do you think he didn't name you as his beneficiary, Dad?"

His dad laughed. "Like you said, son, you're the one who smiled and waved at him. We should never underestimate the power of a smile."

"I guess so," Seth said, suddenly feeling worn out. He struggled to his feet. "I think I'll go up to my room now."

"Looks like we're on our own for dinner."

"Grilled cheese sandwiches it is, then," Seth said, knowing that that was his dad's go-to meal when the cooking fell to him.

Seth was halfway up the stairs when another thought occurred to him. He went back downstairs.

His dad had reclined again and his eyes were closed.

"Dad?"

His dad's eyes blinked open. "Yes, son?"

"I probably shouldn't tell Collin about Grandma and Mr. Garber, should I?"

His dad pressed his lips together; he nodded. "I think it would be best for the time being to keep this to ourselves. Let's give the family time to deal with the emotional fallout from this, especially your grandmother."

"Okay, Dad," Seth said, though he wasn't at all sure what his dad meant by "emotional fallout."

30

SETH HEARD A KNOCK at the front door. It was the last weekend before school was to start, and he'd just gotten home from Beaver Cove, where he and Collin had spent the morning joyously splashing around in their favorite swimming hole—Seth's favorite anyway, because it had the distinct advantage of not being over his head.

If Seth had had his way, he and Collin would have spent the entire day at the cove. Once school began, free time would be at a premium. Then fall would set in, which meant cool days and rain. The window for warm-weather outdoor activities was quickly closing.

But a morning's worth of fun was all they could fit in that day. Collin had to be home by noon. His family was driving down to Azalea to attend the wedding of one of his older cousins. "Yuck!" Collin had said. "I hate weddings. They're so sappy."

The boys had to ride their bikes back from the cove at full sprint so Collin wouldn't be late. Seth had been home just long enough to wolf down a ham sandwich and a glass of milk when he heard the knock.

"See who it is, Seth?" his mother hollered from the laundry room.

"Are you expecting someone?"

"No."

"Where's Dad?"

"In his workshop."

"Where's Baylie?"

"On a field trip to Wildlife Safari with her Brownie troop."

When Seth opened the front door, he was surprised at the figure standing there. This far out of town, not many people came to the door without calling first. Sometimes the Jehovah's Witnesses ventured out this far, and he knew them right away by the Bibles they carried and the pamphlets about heaven and hell. And occasionally someone appeared on their doorstep who was lost and looking for directions. But the man standing in front of him wasn't carrying a Bible, and he didn't look lost.

He looked Asian. He had dark hair and almond-shaped eyes. But he had lighter skin and was taller than Seth would have expected an Asian man to be. He was wearing gray slacks and a short-sleeved dress shirt. The man made a slight bow. "I'm sorry to intrude on your day," he said with a barely noticeable foreign accent. "Is this the home of Seth Roberson?"

Seth took a step back, unnerved by the man's formality and the mention of his name. "Mom!" he hollered.

The man made no move to enter or leave.

When Seth's mother didn't appear, he called out

to her again, more loudly.

"What is it?" she said, puffing as she came up behind him. "Oh, hello," she said to the man at the door.

Again, he bowed. "Mrs. Roberson?"

"Yes."

"My name is Hanh Nguyen, and I'm here to speak with you and your husband."

"What about?"

"Henry Garber."

Seth's mother stared at the man inquisitively. "Henry Garber? Why would you want to speak with us about him?"

The man didn't hesitate to answer. "Because I am his son."

Now it was her turn to holler. "David!"

"He can't hear you, Mom. He's in his shop."

His mother flapped her hands. "Well—go get him."

Seth turned on his heels and ran through the house and out the back door. When he returned with his dad, he saw that a standoff had played out at the front door. Neither Seth's mother nor the man had budged.

"What's going on, dear?" Seth's dad said.

"David," Seth's mother said in a skeptical tone, "this man would like to speak with us. He says he's Henry Garber's son."

Seth's dad regarded the man through narrowed eyes. "That's an interesting assertion, Mr. . . .?"

"Nguyen—Hanh Nguyen."

"Well, Mr. Nguyen, would you care to explain?"

Hanh Nguyen nodded. "Very much so. If I could

have a few minutes of your time, I would greatly appreciate it."

Seth's dad craned his neck as he peered out the open doorway. Seth followed his gaze. Parked in the driveway was a late-model sedan with an Oregon license plate.

"I think we can spare a few minutes," his dad said. "Laura, why don't you and Seth show our guest into the living room while I step outside and brush the sawdust off my clothes."

Seth's mother glared at Hanh Nguyen for an uncomfortable moment—uncomfortable for Seth anyway—before responding. "This way," she said.

Once they were all seated in the living room, Seth on the sofa with his parents and Hanh Nguyen in an armchair on the opposite side of a coffee table, the conversation resumed. "I realize," said Mr. Nguyen, "that my claim to be Henry Garber's son must come as a shock to you."

"We've received more than a few shocks lately," Seth's dad said. "What's one more?"

His mother frowned. "David, surely you don't believe what he's saying." She made a scornful noise similar to the sound of someone lifting the pull tab on a soda can. "He's probably one of those . . . you know . . . one of those people who go around trying to claim a share of someone else's inheritance."

"Mrs. Roberson," said Hanh Nguyen with a polite smile, "I assure you that I'm not after anything, much less someone's inheritance. Though it's true that I obtained Seth's name and address by examining a copy of Henry Garber's will at your courthouse."

Seth's mother wagged her head at her husband. "You see? He *is* after something."

"Please, Mrs. Roberson, if you will allow me to explain, the reason for my visit will become clear, and you'll see that my intentions are honorable."

"Let him speak, Laura," Seth's dad said. "Then we can judge his intentions for ourselves."

"Thank you," said Mr. Nguyen. "That's most gracious of you." He clasped his hands together and spoke earnestly. "Please know that I work for the Vietnam National Administration of Tourism, which has launched an international marketing campaign to boost tourism to Vietnam. I've been assigned to promote tourism to my country from within the U.S. market. Earlier this year, to fulfill my duties, I came to America, where I've been working out of the Consulate General of Vietnam in San Francisco.

"More recently, in late June to be exact, I came to the Pacific Northwest to attend a transpacific tourism conference in Portland. The day prior to that conference, I paid a visit to your town. The events that occurred during that visit, and a subsequent one, have brought me to your door today. And again," he said, nodding respectfully, "I apologize for this intrusion into your lives. But I have a story to tell you that will explain everything—a story I believe you'll want to hear."

He reached into his pants pocket. "But first, I'd like to show you something by way of introduction." He withdrew a coin-shaped object. It was bronze and had decorative etching on it. He handed it to Seth's dad.

His dad held the object up to the sunlight flooding

in through the living room window as he examined it. To Seth, it looked like one of those medals hung around the necks of victorious athletes at the Olympic Games, only smaller.

"What is it?" his dad asked.

"It's a Saint Christopher medallion. Are you familiar with Saint Christopher?"

"Can't say that I am."

"Saint Christopher is the patron saint of travelers. If you look closely, you'll see a figure etched on the face of the medallion. That's a caricature of the saint. A child clings to his back. According to legend, Saint Christopher carried a child whose identity he did not know across a river to safety. Only then did the child reveal himself as Christ. Images of Saint Christopher are often worn or carried by people as good luck charms. An American sailor who fought in Vietnam carried this one. His initials are inscribed on the back."

Seth's dad turned the medallion over and studied the inscription, the expression on his face changing suddenly—like the moment sunlight breaks through clouds—from inquisitive to enlightened. His hand clenched around the medallion.

"What is it, David?" Seth's mother asked.

Seth's dad fastened his gaze on their guest. "Mr. Nguyen, I have no doubt that you have a fascinating story to relate, and I'm eager to hear it. But would you be so kind as to hold off briefly on telling it? I'd like my mother to hear it as well. We can call her and she can be here shortly. Would that be all right with you?"

"Most certainly," said Hanh Nguyen. "I was hoping

you would make such a suggestion."

"Laura," Seth's dad said, pocketing the medallion as he rose from his chair, "would you please make the call? In the meantime, Seth and I will take Mr. Nguyen out to my shop and show him my latest project."

Seth's mother looked bewildered. She opened her mouth as if to speak, but didn't. Then, as if some silent communication had passed between his parents, she went to make the call.

31

GRANDMA CLAIRE'S HANDS TREMBLED as she examined the Saint Christopher medallion and read aloud the inscription on the back: "*HTG, go with God.*" She shook her head. "I don't understand," she said, addressing Hanh Nguyen. "How did you . . . where did you . . . get this medallion?"

The Roberson family, minus Baylie, had reassembled in the living room, along with Mr. Nguyen.

"This medallion was given to me by my mother," said Hanh Nguyen, "who possessed it for many years, since 1971 to be exact. But I see from your reaction that you know who it once belonged to."

Seth's grandmother nodded forlornly. "Yes, this is the good luck charm my mother gave Henry in 1970, the day he left for his tour of duty in Vietnam. When he returned, he said that he'd lost it. He didn't say how or where. And I thought, 'Well, what does it matter? It kept him safe long enough to get home from the war in one piece.'"

"Whether or not it was the medallion that kept him safe, I don't know," said Hanh Nguyen. "But I *can* tell you how it came into my mother's hands."

"I'd very much like to hear that," Seth's grand-mother replied.

Seth was equally eager to hear the man's story. After all, it was his grandfather's medallion they were talking about!

Hanh Nguyen sat mutely for a time with his head bowed, as if in meditation. "What I'm about to tell you," he said, lifting his gaze, "was told to me by my dear mother, who witnessed these events that took place before I was born. But please allow me first to set the scene, because history—especially one's personal history—must be seen in context to be understood.

"In 1971," he said, "my mother's family lived in a small village along the Bassac River in Vietnam, a branch of the expansive Mekong River. My mother, Bui, was eighteen years old at the time. She was unmarried, but only because her arranged marriage had been postponed when her husband-to-be was pressed into service by the South Vietnamese army. Bui and her younger siblings lived with their parents and grandparents and other members of the extended family—aunts and uncles and cousins—in thatched huts along the river. They were simple people, fishermen and farmers and craftsmen.

"Like the Mekong and its other branches, the Bassac was a busy river—full of boats used for commerce as well as personal travel. Fishermen plied the waters. Farmers and other tradesmen used the river to transport their goods to market. The river is shallow, so the boats had flat bottoms. They were made of bamboo and reeds. Sampans, Westerners call them. Some of the bigger boats had canopies and were motorized. The sampans came and went along the river day and night. It's much the same today.

"But in 1971 a war was going on, one that had been in progress for many years. South Vietnamese rebels, known as the Viet Cong, supported by the North Vietnamese military, were warring against the South Vietnam government. And as I'm sure you know, the American military was fighting on the side of the government of South Vietnam.

"It was critical to the war effort, and to the livelihood of the South Vietnamese people, to keep the Mekong River system open for commerce and safe travel. So, during this long war, one job of the U.S. Navy was to patrol the rivers of South Vietnam to keep them secure and to prevent the enemy from using them for transporting troops, munitions, and supplies.

"To do this, the navy used special riverboats with relatively flat bottoms that allowed them to operate in shallow water. They had big engines and could speed up and down the river. Though not heavily armored, the boats were mounted with machine guns and grenade launchers so they could engage with the enemy when necessary.

"Each boat had a four-person crew, including the captain, plus an interpreter. They generally operated in pairs under the command of a patrol officer who rode on one of the boats. They patrolled day and night, because—as we know—the enemy never sleeps.

"The American riverboat crews routinely stopped

and boarded Vietnamese sampans, inspected their cargo, and checked the papers of those on board. Most of the traffic they came upon was legitimate—fishermen hard at work or locals going between villages for commerce or on personal business.

"But sometimes the American sailors, in searching a boat, would discover contraband—munitions or other illegal goods—hidden in the cargo. Or they might find that the papers of some of those aboard weren't in order, leading them to suspect that they had discovered enemy soldiers attempting to infiltrate the South. When this happened, the patrol officer would radio his command center with a request for bigger boats with more men and firepower to come and assist them.

"At other times, the American riverboats encountered trouble they hadn't seen coming. On routine patrol, they might suddenly take fire from enemy fighters hidden in the dense foliage along the riverbanks. Or sometimes things would seem okay when they approached a Vietnamese sampan, but as they prepared to board it guns would appear without warning from under the boat's canopy and a firefight would ensue. In these situations, the riverboat's patrol officer, in addition to requesting more naval firepower, might also call for helicopter gunships—attack helicopters—to come to their aid.

"Sadly, help didn't always arrive in time. Many American riverboats were sunk by the enemy. American lives were lost, and sometimes the locals were caught in the crossfire and became casualties. The job of the riverboat navy was very dangerous but necessary for the war effort."

"Yes," Grandma Claire said, "I'm aware of much of this. That's why I worried so about Henry, because he served on one of the riverboats. They called themselves 'the brown-water navy.'"

"Very appropriate," said Hanh Nguyen, "since the waters of the Mekong Delta can be quite muddy. And yes, I was about to come to Seaman Henry Garber. But before I continue, could I possibly have a glass of water?"

"I think we could all use something to drink," Seth's dad said. "Laura, don't we have some iced tea in the refrigerator and a store of Girl Scout cookies in a cupboard somewhere?"

Seth was fascinated by what he was hearing about the war in Vietnam and couldn't help but wonder where all this was leading. But he was more than willing to wait to find out if it meant a chance to consume some Girl Scout cookies. His parents had bought a number of boxes this year because Baylie's Brownie troop was selling them.

"I'll get a pitcher and glasses," his mother said, and Grandma Claire went with her into the kitchen.

Seth hopped up and followed. "I'll get the cookies." He knew exactly which cupboard they were in.

32

SETH ATE A TAGALONG and a Samoa and was reaching for a Trefoil. "Last one," his mother said. She picked up the platter of assorted cookies and held it out to Hanh Nguyen.

"They're delightful," he said, "but I've had enough, thank you. And I should go on with my story."

"Please do," Seth's dad said.

Mr. Nguyen drank the last of his tea and set the glass down on the coffee table. "As I said, my family consisted of fishermen, farmers, and craftsmen. They lived off the bounty of the land and the river. What they didn't need from what they caught, harvested, and crafted, they traded at a floating market on the river some distance upstream. In exchange for their goods, they received desired commodities such as spices, sauces, soap, fabric, cookware, and the like.

"The periodic boat trips to the market were family events for several reasons. Many hands were needed to load and off-load the cargo to be traded. Also, it was a chance for everyone to break away from their routines for a day. And for the children, there was the excitement of a boat ride and a trip to the market, where they could count on receiving a treat. By children, I mean my mother, Bui, who was the oldest, her three younger siblings, and her many cousins.

"To take all the cargo and passengers, four boats were needed. Because my great-grandfather's fishing boat was the largest and had a canopy, it would carry the bulk of the cargo and most of the children, who adored their grandfather and wanted to ride with him. Additionally, Great-grandfather's sampan had an outboard motor, while the smaller sampans were propelled by men using long oars.

"The trips always began early in the day, with the loading of the boats at sunrise. On the day I speak of—as my mother tells it—everything went well and they were on the river before the sun had chased away the morning mist. As usual, the weather was warm and sticky.

"They made it to the market in good time. Goods were off-loaded and exchanged. The men had the pleasure of smoking and drinking with compatriots from villages farther up the river. The women browsed the market stalls for items they desired. And the children got their treats—mango cakes, fruit candies, sweet corn pudding. Everyone felt the joy of a successful trip to market.

"The sun was hanging low in the sky when everyone reboarded for the journey home. The mood was jubilant. The return trip would require less effort because the downstream flow of the river would aid them. And the younger children, full of sweets and worn down by their play on the market docks, would soon give in to sleep.

"And so it went. By the time the family's small fleet of sampans was within a few kilometers of our village, darkness had settled over the river. It had been a fine trip, and the adults shared a sense of satisfaction that everything had gone well. But that was about to change."

As he continued, Hanh Nguyen's voice softened, and Seth found himself leaning forward so as not to miss a word of the man's story.

"The change came," said Hanh Nguyen, "when at a bend in the river the little flotilla was approached by two American riverboats. My great-grandfather was unconcerned. He was a true patriot of the South, a veteran of the board-and-search procedures. He had nothing to fear from a search, as he always ensured that no weapons or other contraband made its way aboard any boat under his command, and that all transport and identification papers were in order.

"The American riverboats came along either side of the cluster of sampans. An interpreter on one of the patrol boats exchanged words with my great-grandfather, who as requested handed over the paperwork showing the purpose of the trip and the list of passengers. The patrol officer, with the interpreter's assistance, examined the documents. Ultimately, he decided to have Great-grandfather's fishing boat boarded and searched.

"Two American sailors came aboard, while the remaining sailors, their weapons at the ready, maintained defensive positions on the riverboats. One sailor began examining the cargo, while the second inspected the sampan's interior, looking for hidden compartments or anything out of the ordinary. Bui was there with the other children. Despite her assurances that the Americans were friendly, the children were frightened. She gathered them around her and did her best to calm them.

"Following an initial search, one member of the boarding party called back to the patrol officer, informing him that besides my great-grandfather and a helmsman there were only women and children aboard, and miscellaneous personal goods—the cloth and spices and wares the family had purchased at the market.

"Unconvinced, the patrol officer ordered a more thorough search. The American sailors aboard the sampan were about to obey his orders when suddenly there was a loud explosion followed by a huge splash near one of the patrol boats. A rocket-propelled grenade launched from the riverbank had just missed its target.

"Simultaneously, machine-gun fire erupted from both sides of the river, striking the patrol boats as well as the sampans. More explosions followed as more rockets were launched.

"Terrified, those in the sampans dropped to the deck. The children in the big sampan cried out in fear, and their mothers, most of whom were on the smaller boats, cried out as well, afraid not only for themselves but for their children.

"As soon as the assault from the riverbanks began, the gunners on the American patrol boats returned fire. But they were at a disadvantage because they were receiving fire from two sides, with my family's sampans sandwiched between them. There was no doubt in anyone's mind what had happened: the Viet Cong had staged an ambush and had brought plenty of firepower.

"The captain of the patrol boat whose men were on Great-grandfather's sampan yelled at them to get back aboard the riverboat. But before they could do so, a rocket struck low on the side of the big sampan. A thunderous explosion tore a gaping hole in the hull, causing the boat to list and take on water.

"To save himself, one member of the boarding party dove into the river, swam back to his boat, and with assistance reboarded it. But the other sailor, responding to the plight of the sampan's occupants—mostly children—began helping my great-grandfather transfer passengers from the bigger boat to the three smaller sampans. Lifting the children by their underarms, they flung them into the waiting arms of the adults on the other boats.

"The situation became more urgent when the big sampan caught fire and began to sink into the dark, muddy waters of the Bassac. Great-grandfather and the American sailor worked frantically to shift all the children to the smaller vessels.

"Unfortunately, time wasn't on their side. Without warning, the bigger sampan—now in its death throes—capsized, sending the remaining children aboard plunging into the river, along with Great-grandfather and the American sailor. Men from the smaller sampans jumped into the river to rescue the children floundering in the water.

"Clinging to the dislodged canopy of his sinking

boat, my great-grandfather watched this disaster play out. He also foresaw a greater calamity. Intentional or not, machine-gun fire continued to strike the sides of the smaller sampans, while rockets landed all around them. The men, women, and children in those boats—three generations of Great-grandfather's family—were in danger of being lost forever, sent by a heartless enemy to a watery grave.

"In a desperate move to avoid this final insult, Great-grandfather ordered the oarsmen of the remaining sampans, still afloat but precariously weighted down with passengers, to abandon the rescue effort and retreat down river.

"At the same time, my great-grandmother, aboard one of those sampans, was screaming for the oarsmen to wait until everyone from the sinking boat had been rescued.

"But Great-grandfather knew that if they delayed even for a minute, his entire family would be lost. 'Go!' he commanded, waving the boats away from the conflict. The oarsmen obeyed; ignoring Great-grandmother's cries, they worked their oars feverishly to escape.

"The captains of the two American riverboats had the same idea. But as they were attempting their retreat, one of the patrol boats received a direct hit from a rocket and had to be abandoned. Fortunately, its crew managed to jump aboard the surviving riverboat, which then sped away while still taking fire.

"Somehow, in the darkness and smoke and confusion of battle, the three imperiled sampans slipped away from danger. Behind them, the gunfire finally subsided, and the rocket launchers went silent.

"Bui was one of those who had been saved, along with her siblings, except for the youngest, a brother. He was three years old and his name was Coduca. 'Where is Coduca?' my mother cried out, but nobody knew. 'We must go back and get Coduca!'

"'We cannot go back!' came a booming voice out of the night. It was my great-grandfather. He was still in the water, clinging to the stern of one of the sampans. Two men rushed to him and pulled him into the boat. 'If we go back,' he said, 'we will all die.'

"My great-grandfather was wise. What he suspected and later confirmed was that the ambush had been a setup. Someone in our village, a northern sympathizer, had planted false information with the American military about alleged smuggling activity involving my great-grandfather.

"My family's market trip had provided the perfect opportunity to complete the betrayal. The culprit had notified the Americans of the timing of the trip. They had also informed the Viet Cong. This allowed the enemy to stake out positions along the river so they could attack the American riverboats when they intercepted my family's little flotilla. To hide the fact that my great-grandfather wasn't carrying contraband, the Viet Cong were just as intent on sinking his boats as they were on killing the Americans. That's why the sampans were taking so much fire."

"But what has all of this to do with Henry Garber?" Seth's grandmother asked.

The same question was on Seth's mind as well, although he suspected that he already knew the answer.

33

"As I recounted earlier," said Hanh Nguyen, "during the firefight only one of the American sailors who'd boarded my great-grandfather's sampan made it back safely aboard his patrol boat." He paused, as if to allow this detail to resurface in the minds of his listeners.

"Yes, I recall," said Grandma Claire, her voice tentative, expectant.

"As it so happened," said Mr. Nguyen, "the sailor who did not reboard the American riverboat, but who willingly stayed on Great-grandfather's sampan to help rescue the children, was none other than Seaman Henry Garber."

"My God," Seth's grandmother exclaimed, covering her mouth but not the depth of her emotion. "What happened to Henry?"

"Indeed," said Hanh Nguyen, "that is the crux of my story."

He sighed deeply before continuing. "In the chaos of combat, with the sinking of Great-grandfather's sampan and the family's frantic escape, there was no way to know who had survived and who hadn't.

"Only after the damaged, overburdened sampans limped back to our village and the passengers were off-loaded could an accurate head count be taken. To everyone's surprise, only five members of our extended family were unaccounted for—an aunt of my mother's, two of her uncles (one a great-uncle), an eleven-year-old girl cousin, and my mother's three-year-old brother, Coduca.

"My grandmother was beside herself with grief and anger. Her agony getting the best of her, she demanded that Great-grandfather send a search party back at once to look for her youngest son and the others who were missing.

"Great-grandfather refused. He knew that by then the bigger American riverboats, the ones called monitors, would have arrived on the scene. And helicopter gunships would be patrolling the shores in search of the Viet Cong attackers. 'We must wait until the Americans are gone,' he said. 'They think we are smugglers. Besides, it is too dark. We will only put more lives in danger.'

"But Great-grandfather was not without empathy, and he felt deeply the loss of any family member. The next morning at first light, in one of the smaller sampans, he headed out with a search party of six men.

"Always watchful, they made their way up the river to the site of the melee. There they came upon broken and burnt debris along the riverbank and, sticking up out of the water, the communications dome of the sunken American riverboat. They also found, caught in the brush along the bank, two bodies, that of the aunt and an uncle. Solemnly, they loaded the bodies aboard the sampan before continuing their search.

"In the hours that followed, they combed the riverbanks without finding any trace of the other missing family members. Feeling defeated and dreading having to face the immediate family of the missing, Great-grandfather ordered the search party back to their village.

"They had gone only a short distance when they heard a faint voice calling out: '*Ông nôi* . . . *Ông nôi* . . . Grandfather . . . Grandfather.' Anxiously, the men rowed toward the voice. They ran their boat into the brush and leaped out onto the marshy soil.

"The vegetation was dense and knotted, and it took them some time to find Coduca ensnared in a tangle of mangrove roots. He was wet and muddy and had scrapes on his face and other exposed parts of his body. Great-grandfather snatched him up in his arms. With tears in his eyes, he clasped him to his chest as the party retraced their steps to the sampan.

"But, in agitation, the boy pointed back to where they had found him. '*Đàn ông* . . . *đàn ông*,' he said, repeating the Vietnamese word for man.

"'What man? *Ông Câu*?' Great-grandfather asked, meaning great-uncle. Coduca, he thought, must be referring to his wife's missing brother. But Coduca fretfully shook his head and continued pointing and repeating himself. Great-grandfather began to wonder whether Viet Cong soldiers were still in the area.

Against his better judgment, he directed the search party to turn back and look for the man his grandson was referring to.

"Once they got back to the spot where they had found Coduca, it didn't take them long to locate the man. He lay motionless, his head barely out of the bog. Little if any life was left in him.

"As they moved closer, they saw another figure lying next to him, obviously lifeless. It was the body of Bui's eleven-year-old cousin Linh. One of the men in the search party was her father. He ran to her, lifted her up, and cradling her body in his arms, wept bitterly.

"Great-grandfather went over to the male figure. It was the American sailor—the one who had made no attempt to reboard the riverboat but instead had helped Great-grandfather save the children in the sinking sampan."

"Oh . . . *my Henry*," Seth's grandmother muttered and began sobbing softly.

"Yes," said Hanh Nguyen with compassion in his voice, "your Henry." He waited for her to compose herself.

"Please go on," she said as she wiped tears from her eyes.

Mr. Nguyen nodded. "For your sake and mine, we're nearing the end of my story."

He continued: "Great-grandfather knelt beside the American sailor. The man's uniform was crusted with mud. His face was deathly pale. A gash on his head just above the hairline oozed blood. Leaning in closer, Great-grandfather noted a slight rise and fall of the man's chest. He was alive.

"'What shall we do with him?' asked a member of the search party.

"Great-grandfather didn't know the answer to this question. The American sailor had risked his life to save members of his family. He had succeeded in rescuing little Coduca and had done his best to save young Linh. But what to do with him? Left where he was, he would surely die—of blood loss and exposure. Yet taking him back to the village could mean a death sentence for the entire Nguyen family, as well as for the sailor.

"There was a traitor in the village; Great-grandfather was certain of that. The traitor would no doubt notify the Viet Cong, who would kill or capture the American and take revenge on those who had harbored him. The safest thing to do was to notify the American military anonymously of the sailor's whereabouts and hope they would find him before he bled to death or word of his presence reached the Viet Cong.

"In the end, my great-grandfather rejected that notion. He was a man of honor and integrity. He knew when he had incurred a great debt and was required to repay that debt. He told his men to take Coduca, poor lifeless Linh, and the bodies of the aunt and uncle back to the village. Then two of the men were to come back with a stretcher. They were also to bring clean cloth, healing ointment, and three days' worth of food and water for four people. And they were to bring Bui, my mother, with them.

"The men did as they were told.

"Great-grandfather stayed with the American seaman. He propped him up and, when the man came to, gave him coconut juice to drink and bits of papaya to eat.

"When the two men returned with Bui and the items requested, Great-grandfather instructed her to use the cloth and ointment to bandage the sailor's head wound. Then he told his men what to do. They were to put the American on the stretcher and carry him inland to the home of one of Great-grandfather's cousins. They were to take Bui with them to tend to the man during the journey.

"If he died along the way, they were to bury him and return home. Otherwise, they were to continue on, deliver their patient, and then return. Bui was to stay with the American at the cousin's house. If he died, she was to send word of his death, and men would be sent to escort her home. If he lived, she was to stay and care for him until he was well enough to make his way, with the cousin's guidance, back to the safety of an American military outpost.

"As you know, the American sailor—Henry Garber—lived. But it would be weeks before he was fit enough to travel.

"During this time, my mother nursed him, fed him, changed his dressing, and prayed for his recovery. She also grew very fond of him, and he of her. On the night before the American's departure from the cousin's house, my mother lay with him. That's when I was conceived, unknown to the sailor.

"The next morning, as Seaman Garber prepared for his journey, he and my mother were both in tears. But they knew it could end no other way. Their union was an accident of circumstance—to say nothing of the fact that he already had a family in America that, despite his passing liaison with my mother, he loved very much.

"The last thing he did before he left was to press into my mother's hand the very Saint Christopher medallion you now hold in yours, Mrs. Roberson. 'It will keep you safe,' he told her. And for these many years, it has."

Seth's grandmother clutched the medallion to her breast, more tears springing from her eyes. "Dear, dear Henry. No wonder you came back from the war a different person."

34

"I HAVE NO DOUBT that Seaman Garber was haunted
for a lifetime by what he experienced during the
war," said Hanh Nguyen. He faltered; his face grew
ashen. "Now I owe it to you to relate the details of
my one and only encounter with him, an encounter
that will haunt *me* for the rest of *my* life."

In the silence that followed this remark, Seth
could only sit and wonder what Mr. Nguyen was
talking about. His encounter with Henry Garber?
What encounter? And what *details* could be so awful
as to haunt the man for a lifetime?

"It was my mother," Hanh Nguyen went on to say,
"who proposed I launch an effort to locate Seaman
Garber.

"'To what purpose?' I asked her. 'He doesn't know
I exist. After all these years, what good could come of
my contacting him? And what about Minh? Have
you taken his feelings into account?' Minh was the
man my mother married not long after my birth. He
was a good man who raised me as his own son.

"But my mother was insistent that I reach out to

Henry Garber. 'He fathered you,' she said. 'He deserves to know that he has such a fine son as you.'

"Reluctantly, then, I set about discovering his whereabouts. I did this with the assistance of an American tourism contact whose brother works for the U.S. Department of Veterans Affairs. He was able to access the records of current VA patients. Through those records, I obtained Henry Garber's address. Even then, I felt little incentive to follow up, so I put the matter aside.

"But when my mother learned of my upcoming assignment to America, the issue reemerged. Again she urged me to connect with Henry Garber and reveal myself as his son.

"I was still skeptical. 'He won't believe me,' I told her. 'Show him this medallion,' she said, placing it in my hand, 'and he will know you are who you say you are.' Not wanting to defy her wishes, I vowed to make the effort.

"My job at the consulate in San Francisco is quite demanding of my time, however, and it was some months before I had an opportunity to keep that promise. Only when I was slated, in late June, to attend the tourism conference in Portland, did I have my chance.

"I flew to Portland two days before the conference was to begin. The next morning, I rented a car and made the three-hour drive to Roseburg. I used my GPS to locate Henry Garber's hillside home.

"Yet even as I pulled to a stop in front of his house, I wasn't convinced I was doing the right thing. I thought that even if he believed what I was about to tell him, he would have no feelings for me in his heart. How could he? So many years had passed since his service in Vietnam. And who wants to remember what happened during war? But I had promised my mother.

"I knocked on the front door. Receiving no answer, I knocked again. Still no response. Honestly, I was relieved to find no one home.

"I walked back to my car and would have driven away had I not taken in the view of the beautiful valley below. There, a shimmering pond was surrounded by broad meadows dotted with country homes. Focusing my gaze on the pond, I observed a small boat on the water and, sitting in it, a lone man.

"I'm not sure why, but I was drawn by a strong feeling of kinship to the man in the boat. Perhaps it was because of my family's heritage of fishing in the rivers of my home country. It could have been any man out there on that pond. But I thought, *Could this be Seaman Garber?*

"On impulse, I decided to find out. Seeing no way to drive to the pond from where I stood, I trekked down the wooded slope on foot. I crossed a gravel road, scaled a sagging fence, and made my way through brush and berry vines to reach the pond.

"Coming upon a clearing at the water's edge, I saw the man in the boat rowing toward shore. He was approaching the bank. There was a dog in the boat with him. I waved my arms and hailed the man. 'Good day,' I said. 'Do you happen to know a man named Henry Garber?'

"He stopped rowing and looked up at me in bewilderment. I repeated my question more loudly, thinking he hadn't heard me the first time.

"The man's reaction dumbfounded me. Abruptly, he stood up in his boat, causing it to teeter. Shuffling his feet in an attempt to maintain his balance, he stumbled over something. He lurched sideways, hung briefly over the edge of the boat with one foot in the air, then fell into the water.

"Dismayed, I waded into the pond to assist him. The water was shallow but the bottom boggy, and I struggled to keep my footing.

"As I made my way toward the man, he stood up in the water, a look of terror on his face. He backpedaled, nearly falling, then reeled around and strode away from me.

"Approaching his boat, I saw that the dog had managed to stay in it. *Should I rescue the dog?* I pondered. As I came closer, it barked at me with bared teeth. Even though it wasn't a big or vicious-looking dog, I backed off.

"I was at a loss to understand what was happening. In my heart, I was sure I'd stumbled upon my own father, but for some reason I had frightened him. I took several more clumsy steps toward him as he tramped his way into deeper water. I cupped my hands around my mouth and called out, 'Please stop. I only want to talk to you.'

"But he continued thrashing through the water with his back to me, and I realized I was only driving him farther away. Disheartened, I gave up the pursuit and made my way back to shore. I stood on the bank and watched as he lumbered out toward the middle of the pond.

"At times he'd stop and gaze about, agitated, as if desperate to find something or someone. Then he would dive under the surface, staying there longer than I imagined a man could, only to surface and repeat his frenzied behavior. In the boat, the dog continued to bark. It jumped and spun and tossed itself around wildly, mirroring its master's hysteria yet always staying in the boat.

"I watched this spectacle continue until the only thing to do was leave the scene, hoping this would bring an end to the mania I had somehow incited. Crestfallen, I climbed back up the hill, got into my rental car, and drove back to Portland.

"Alone in my motel room that night, I was heavy hearted. I felt the shame of failing to fulfill my mother's wishes. I was also concerned about the well-being of the man at the pond. I'd been convinced the man was Henry Garber, but now I wasn't so sure. *I should return to Roseburg, I told myself, and make one more effort to contact Seaman Garber.* But how? When? My conference would begin the next day.

"The tourism conference lasted three days, and I was expected back at the consulate the following day. That evening, as I packed for my flight back to San Francisco, I was fraught with anxiety. When would I ever have another chance to carry out my mother's wishes? In despair, I called the consulate and requested a two-day trip extension, telling them I wanted to follow up with some contacts I'd made at the tourism conference. My request was granted.

"Early the next morning, I drove back to Roseburg and made my way to Henry Garber's address. But when I got there, I found the entrance to his driveway blocked by a barricade. Confused, I left my car there and walked up the drive. I was alarmed to see yellow police tape strung around the house. Something terrible had taken place, and it had happened since my earlier visit.

"I didn't know what to do. Should I contact the authorities to find out what had occurred? Or should I simply go home and give up my quest? In truth, I didn't want to do either of these things. What I wanted was to go inside this house and discover what I could about the man who had fathered me.

"So I made what I now know was an irrational decision. No one was around, so I entered the house through the front door, which was easy to open with a credit card. I went through the house in search of clues about Henry Garber's personal life.

"In the living room was a writing desk with a drawer that I supposed might contain correspondence or other papers that would provide the kind of information I sought. I opened the drawer, but it jammed after coming only partially open. I gave the handle a firm tug. The drawer flew open, slid out of its tracks, and dislodged from the desk, spilling its contents onto the floor.

"I was aghast and immediately began working to refit the drawer. Before I could finish, I heard voices coming from outside the front of the house. Fearful of being discovered, I dropped the drawer, ran to the back of the house, and hid in a closet behind some hanging clothes. I had entered the house for honorable reasons, but others might not see it that way.

"For the next while, I waited and listened, doing my best to remain calm. Then my plight became more perilous. People had entered the house. I knew this because I could hear their voices more distinctly now as they moved through the house, at one point entering the room I was in. That's when I realized they were immature voices—likely those of young boys. Knowing this made me less afraid, though no less motivated to escape the situation.

"When the voices trailed off to the front part of the house, I slipped out of the closet and rushed to the window in the room. I slid it open, pushed out the screen, climbed out, and dropped to the ground.

"I'd barely gotten my feet under me when I was confronted by a dog—the same dog I had faced off with at the pond. It snarled at me and barked angrily as before. In a panic, I ran as fast as I could around the house and down the driveway to my car and drove away.

"The following day, I flew back to San Francisco and returned to my job at the consulate. But as I went about my work, I was preoccupied by thoughts of Henry Garber. Weighing heavily on me was my failure to connect with him. Even more troubling was the lingering image of the police tape around his house.

"Anxious to know what had happened, I went online and read recent issues of your local newspaper. There I learned that two boys had discovered Henry Garber's body in a pond—the very pond, I was sure, where I had seen him. I was shocked and saddened and overwhelmed with guilt, convinced I was somehow responsible for my own father's death.

"Even when I read in a later article that his death had been ruled an accidental drowning, I felt the crushing weight of self-blame. *I must inform the authorities of my involvement,* I told myself, and I resolved to do so, but only when I could do it in person.

"Regrettably, my job at the consulate allows me little free time, and this is the first opportunity I've had to travel back to your town. It will also be the last, I'm afraid, as I've been called back to my home country to oversee a new tourism program."

Hanh Nguyen sighed. "And you should know that before coming to your home today, I stopped at your local sheriff's office. I identified myself and recounted for them the incident at the pond that day in late June. I explained the reason for my effort to contact Henry Garber and for, later, entering his house.

"The authorities there checked my passport, made the necessary calls to verify my consular status, and released me. All the evidence, they said, indicated that Henry Garber's death was an accident, and my story only supported this. A deputy there, a man named Waller, suggested I seek you out and tell you my story."

Hanh Nguyen pressed his palms together and dipped his head deferentially. "I pray that I have made the right decision in doing so."

Seth's dad spoke up. "You did indeed, Mr. Nguyen. And the police were right not to detain you. Henry Garber's death wasn't your fault. It was the fault of the war he fought, not just in Vietnam but every day of his life since then. We—you and I—lost a father we never knew. And now we can only hope that in death Henry Garber found the peace he couldn't find in life."

"Then let it be so," said Hanh Nguyen.

35

SETH'S GRANDMOTHER SAT QUIETLY, head bowed, seemingly lost in thought. Hanh Nguyen spoke to her directly now. "Mrs. Roberson, I know that what I've told you today has been difficult for you to hear. But I hope you will find comfort in one last element of my story that I would like to share with you.

"I draw your attention once more to the Saint Christopher medallion you hold—to the image of the saint depicted thereon. On his back clings the child who, according to legend, Saint Christopher carried across a river to safety—the child who later revealed himself as Christ.

"There are many coincidences in this world for which there are no explanations, and this may be one of them. Nevertheless, I think you should know that when, in the heat of battle, Seaman Garber rescued little Coduca from the muddy waters of the Bassac River, he was saving the life of a child whose name means 'blessed.'

"Furthermore, this same Coduca—my mother's little brother and my uncle—is today a revered monk at one of the oldest Buddhist temples in Vietnam."

Hanh Nguyen's face radiated empathy. "So, yes, it's true that the Vietnam War had a devastating impact on your Henry and his family here in America. That tragedy can't be undone. But it's also true that his heroic actions during the war altered many Vietnamese lives in a profoundly positive and perhaps even miraculous way."

These words left Seth feeling dazed as he struggled to understand the significance of everything he'd just heard. Hanh Nguyen had delivered a powerful story—a story of heroism, of infidelity, and of the long-lasting trauma of war—trauma that in the end had led to Henry Garber's "accidental" death. The story had rewritten the personal histories of everyone in the room, and in so doing had upended so much of what they "knew" to be real. For no one was this truer than for Seth's grandmother, and he wondered what her reaction would be.

So, it seemed, did everyone else, for all eyes were on her now. In the hush of the moment, Seth imagined that he could hear a chorus of hearts beating in anticipation of her response.

Slowly she lifted her head. Remnants of blotted tears glistened on her cheeks. She directed her gaze at Hanh Nguyen and smiled bravely. "Thank you, Mr. Nguyen, for coming here today and sharing your story with us. That took courage. Your mother was right—Henry would have wanted to know that he had fathered such an exceptional young man as you. I only wish your meeting with him had turned out differently."

She issued a sigh that seemed to come from deep

within her. "It will take some time for me to process everything you've told us here today. And more time still to put it into proper perspective. But I have no doubt that when I do, I'll be able to achieve a greater understanding and acceptance of a vital chapter of my life than otherwise would have been possible. And I thank you for that as well."

Hanh Nguyen rose and bowed deeply. "I'm humbled by your generosity of spirit, Mrs. Roberson. And now, with your permission, I must take my leave. I'm scheduled to fly back to San Francisco this evening."

"I understand," Seth's grandmother said. Her head drooped then, and the light in her eyes dimmed as if she had reentered the cavern of her own thoughts.

Seth's dad stood up. "I'll walk you to your car, Mr. Nguyen."

"Can I come too, Dad?" Seth asked.

"Sure, son."

The three of them went out the front door and walked to the rental car.

"Safe travels," Seth's dad said, extending Hanh Nguyen a hand. "I'm glad we met, despite the unfortunate circumstances. And I sincerely hope our paths cross again someday."

"That is my hope as well," said Hanh Nguyen.

The two men shook hands.

"Do you really have to go back to Vietnam right away?" Seth asked, saddened by the man's departure.

"Yes," said Mr. Nguyen. He laughed. "My mother may have had something to do with that. It seems that she's become quite friendly with the wife of our national director of tourism. What do you call it here in America? *Pulling strings?*"

"That's precisely what we call it," Seth's dad said.

They all laughed. But as Hanh Nguyen opened the driver's door of his rental car, the sadness Seth had felt returned.

"Wait!" called a voice from behind them.

They turned to see Grandma Claire coming out of the house, Seth's mother at her side. As the two women approached, Seth noted that his grandmother's brave smile had been replaced by a glow that suggested an inner peace.

She embraced Hanh Nguyen in a robust hug. Then she did what Henry Garber had done for Bui Nguyen all those years ago when faced with a final parting: she pressed the Saint Christopher medallion into his hand. "Keep this with you," she said. "And may it always keep you safe."

Hanh Nguyen beamed as he clutched the medallion. "You do me a great honor," he said, bowing once again. Then he shook hands all around, with Seth too. And when he did, Seth returned his bow.

36

SETH JOSTLED HIS WAY down the crowded hallway. It was his first day of middle school. He had survived his morning classes, and now it was lunchtime. Then three more classes in the afternoon before the ending bell. Things were moving so fast he hardly had time to think about anything except what was happening at a given moment.

When he got to his locker, he referred to the numbers written on the back of his hand. *First, to the right two revolutions stopping at the first number; next, to the left a full turn, passing the first number and stopping at the second number; then, back to the right, stopping at the third number.* He was so jittery spinning the number wheel that it took him three attempts to open the locker. He put his three-ring binder inside, took out his lunch bag, and closed the locker. A cacophony of slamming locker doors, shuffling feet, and booming voices echoed down the hallway.

Entering the cafeteria, he was happy to see Collin sitting at a table waving at him. They had only one class together in the morning, social studies, and one in the afternoon, wellness. Collin had already gone through the lunch line and was attacking his food as if he hadn't eaten in a week. Seth preferred to bring his lunch.

He set his bag on the table. "I gotta buy milk." When he returned, milk carton in hand, he sat down next to Collin.

"I already got a ton of math homework," Collin complained through a mouthful of Turkey Chow Mein. "Mr. Tabor is a grumpy goat. Did you like Mrs. Palmer?" She was the social studies teacher.

Seth shrugged. "She's okay."

"Something's wrong with her left eye," Collin said. "It never opens all the way. When she looks at you, she gives you this weird one-eyed squint."

Seth had noticed it too, but he hadn't wanted his noticing to be noticeable, so he'd looked away whenever Mrs. Palmer gazed in his direction. "Maybe she got poked in the eye or something."

Collin wiped his mouth with the back of his hand. "It's creepy all the same."

Seth opened his lunch bag and brought out his peanut butter and jelly sandwich. As he sat eating and listening to Collin's ongoing commentary about each of his morning classes, it occurred to Seth that one thing about middle school was no different from elementary school: it was noisy enough in the cafeteria to burst your eardrums. The scene was barely controlled chaos. It was as if the students had been bound and gagged all morning, and now free of their bonds they felt compelled to yell and laugh and engage in horseplay before being straitjacketed again.

The cafeteria monitors didn't stand a chance against this mob.

"We only get thirty minutes," Collin said, "and that's half gone. Better eat up."

Seth did.

After retrieving his binder from his locker, he trundled down the hall to his math class, arriving seconds before the tardy bell. All the seats in the back were taken, so he had to sit near the front of the room. Math came easily for Seth. He let his mind wander as the teacher spent the entire period reviewing stuff he already knew.

Wellness class was, well, interesting. The teacher talked to them about self-esteem, about how important it was to have a good self-image, and how a bad self-image can lead to problems like depression, drug use, and self-harm. Seth didn't think he had a problem with self-esteem, but he hadn't really given it much thought. He knew there were other kids who were smarter and stronger and better at a lot of things than he was, but it didn't bother him. That's just the way it was.

For the rest of the class time, the teacher had them get construction paper, scissors, glue, and magazines from a table at the back of the room. Then each student was to create a collage of words and pictures that expressed something positive about themselves. Seth wasn't sure he understood what the teacher was getting at, but he cut out some pictures—mostly of outdoor scenes and animals. One had a caption that read, "It's a dog's world, but don't tell the cats." He glued the pictures onto green paper in no particular pattern.

Collin, who was sitting across the aisle from him, dropped his glue stick on the floor. When he reached down to pick it up, he frowned and mouthed to Seth, "I'd rather run laps."

By the time the bell rang for transition to seventh period, Seth felt drained. The day had been a whirl-wind of new experiences and new faces. All his teachers were new to him, and he didn't know most of the kids in his classes because they came from different elementary schools in town. All of this was going to take some getting used to.

He slurped from a drinking fountain on his way to his last class of the day, language arts. He took a seat near the door for a quick getaway at the ending bell. The teacher sat at her desk putting papers into a folder, which she then placed atop other folders. Shortly after the tardy bell rang, she stood up, swept the room with her gaze, and smiled. "Good after-noon, young ladies and young gentlemen."

Two girls rushed in through the door, and the teacher waited for them to find seats. "My name is Mrs. Timmons," she said, "and I'll be your language arts teacher this semester. I suspect that by now, at the end of your first day in middle school, most of you are feeling a bit frazzled. Believe me, things will get better. Before long, you'll be in the swing of things, singing your way through the day like the wrens and robins chirping outside our windows. So let's all relax now, take a big breath, and slow down our heartbeats a few clicks."

Seth took a deep breath. It didn't help. What he needed was for the school day to end.

"Now what I want to do today," Mrs. Timmons

said, "is to introduce you briefly to the subject of language arts. Then we'll have a short writing exercise." She held up her palms in response to the groans that reverberated around the room. "Nothing challenging, I promise you. Just something that will help me get to know you better."

The groaning died down but the collective anxiety that had prompted it hung around like a dark cloud on an otherwise sunny day.

"So what is the discipline we call language arts?" said Mrs. Timmons, powering on. "It is simply the communication of ideas through language. When you talk to your parents or your siblings, you're practicing language arts. When you exchange notes with a friend, you're practicing language arts. When you tell someone about a movie you saw or a book you read, you're practicing language arts.

"In all these instances, and many others in your daily life, you're practicing language arts—that is, you're using words to communicate ideas and to understand the ideas others communicate to you. The goal of this class is to enable you to communicate your ideas as proficiently as possible—in short, to help you become a better communicator. Now that doesn't sound so scary, does it?"

No one responded. "You don't have to all cheer at once," she said with a brittle laugh.

"Okay, as I said, today I'm going to engage you in a little writing exercise, one that will help me get to know you better in two ways. It will tell me something about you as a person, and it will tell me something about your current proficiency in communicating your ideas. So," she said, clapping her hands enthusiastically, "everyone take out a sheet of paper."

Another stir of discontent—grumbles, shifting of desks, scuffing of feet—greeted her directive. Seth didn't contribute to the commotion. He was too tired to get worked up about a writing exercise.

Once again, Mrs. Timmons flourished her palms. "All right, before you all panic, I want to assure you that this is not a test and no grade will be given. This exercise is for fun, and for my enlightenment. All I want you to do is this: write down five things you did this summer. It could be something fun you did. It could be something scary you did. If you went on a trip, it could be something you saw or did on the trip. Just write down whatever comes to mind.

"And don't worry—if you can't think of five things, then give me four, or three. But give me something. The only requirement is that you use complete sentences. Is that clear? Does anyone have any questions?"

A girl at the front of the room asked, "Can we give more than five things?"

"If you'd like."

A boy behind Seth said, "My pencil lead broke. Can I use the pencil sharpener?"

"You may. Now if there are no more questions, please begin your assignment. I suggest that you first take a few minutes to think about what you want to say. You might also want to jot down some notes on a separate sheet of paper to help you order your thoughts before you start writing. And please work quietly so as not to disturb your neighbor.

"When you're done, put your name at the top of

your paper and bring it up to me. Then stay with me until I've had a chance to read what you've written. But don't line up at my desk. Wait for the person ahead of you to take his or her seat before coming up. If there's class time left after you've turned in your paper, you may work on homework from another class."

Seth sat at his desk thinking about what to write. So much had happened over the summer that, in a way, it seemed as if years had passed instead of months. Was he even the same person now? Yes, but surely a different version of himself. For he felt oddly distant from the boy who, with his friend, during those early days of summer, built a raft and floated it upon a pond.

He took up his pencil and began making notes. But calling to mind the summer's events was like untangling a knotted wad of twine, and his paper soon became filled with a disordered heap of recollections—so many that it was hard to know what to tell and what to leave out.

Five things, Mrs. Timmons had said.

He looked over his notes, circled some things and crossed out others. Finally, he took out a clean sheet of paper and began to write. When he was done, he read what he had written:

> *This summer I discovered a dead body floating in a pond. I inherited a house. I found and lost a grandfather. I gained an uncle. And I learned about an illness called post-traumatic stress disorder.*

No one was at Mrs. Timmons's desk, so he went

up and handed her his paper. He stood and waited while she read it. When she was finished, she gazed up at him with a look that drilled right into his heart. "I'm guessing that this was a summer you will never forget."

"Yes, ma'am," he said.

COLLIN WAS WAITING FOR HIM at the lineup of big yellow buses parked along the curb in front of the school. "That one's ours," Collin said, pointing at the third bus in line.

"I forgot to tell you," Seth said. "I'm not riding the bus home on Tuesdays. My dad is picking me up when he gets off work."

"But that's a long time from now. What are you gonna do until then?"

"Visit someone."

"Who?"

"No one you know."

"Then how come you know 'em?"

Seth shrugged. "I just do."

The school buses were filling up with backpack-toting students, many of whom looked as bedraggled as Seth felt. Though now that he was out of class and had somewhere to go that held a different kind of promise, he was feeling more energized.

The bus drivers started their engines. Seth nodded toward the line of buses. "You'd better get on before you get left behind. I'll call you later to see if you need help with your math homework."

Collin punched him on the arm, but not hard enough to hurt. "You better."

Seth shouldered his backpack and headed up the

sidewalk away from the school and the buses. It was just over a mile to his destination. At first, his parents had balked at his request to let him stay after school one day a week. But after some discussion, they agreed he could do so "on a trial basis." His dad had elaborated: "Let's take it a week at a time and see how it goes." That sounded fair to Seth.

School buses passed him on the street now, as did students on bicycles, their legs pumping furiously, as if their happiness depended on their distancing themselves from the classrooms in which they'd been confined for the better part of the day. On the sidewalk, students who lived close enough to the school to walk home formed a fragmented line of pedestrians moving as erratically as birds in frightened flight. Seth fell in with the flow, diverging from it only as his destination dictated.

The notion of how he wanted to spend an hour or so after school one day a week had been squirming in the back of his mind for some time; he had only to let it out. When he did, it felt like the most natural thing in the world.

"Are you sure you want to do this?" his dad had asked him.

"I'm sure, Dad. Why wouldn't I?"

"No reason."

Walking at his natural pace, it took him about fifteen minutes to reach the southern entrance to the Roseburg VA Healthcare System campus. Ahead of him, on his left, was the small cluster of apartment buildings known as Eagle Landing. He entered the complex, found the unit he was looking for, and knocked.

Art Winkelman opened the door. "Good to see you again, Seth."

"Good to see you, Mr. Winkelman."

The old soldier gave a flicker of a smile. "If we're gonna be friends, son, you better start calling me Art."

"Yes, sir," Seth said as he entered the apartment. "I mean, Art."

"Well, that's a start."

Epilogue

SETH WAS IN HIS ROOM doing homework. It was Saturday, so the weekend homework rule was in effect: Friday nights he could work on homework or not, as he chose. But on Saturdays, before he and Collin could meet up for their next adventure, he had to be done (or mostly done) with his homework. No putting it off until Sunday and then having to rush through it. He had read the chapter in his social studies textbook about the Middle Ages in Europe and was completing the related worksheet when he heard a car honk.

His mother called up to him from downstairs. "Seth, your dad's home. Go help him unload."

"Unload what?" All Seth knew was that, according to his mother anyway, his dad had gone off earlier on an errand.

"You'll see."

What Seth saw when he got outside was his dad standing by a back door of his Taurus. When Seth approached, his dad opened the door. "Come on out, boy," he said.

Seth wondered who his dad was talking to. Then it happened—the most wonderful surprise he could ever have imagined. Pond Dog, with that unmistakable Brillo-pad coat, hopped out of the car and onto the driveway. Seth couldn't believe his eyes. He gasped and rushed to the dog.

"It's you! It's really you!" He dropped to his knees and embraced the dog, nuzzling him cheek to muzzle, his heart galloping out of control. He gazed up at his dad. "Dad, how . . .?"

"Ask your mother," his dad said, nodding toward the house. "It was her doing."

Seth glanced back at the house, where his mother stood on the front porch with a big smile on her face.

"It was actually the dog's doing," she told him minutes later. In the excitement of the moment, the family had gathered on the porch. Seth's mom and dad, with Baylie between them, sat on the porch swing, the wooden slats creaking under their weight. Seth, the dog snuggled between his legs, sat on the steps.

"The dog's doing?" Seth said. "What do you mean by that?"

"Well, young man," his mother said lightheartedly, "let me tell you what happened. Yesterday, while you and Baylie were at school, I got a very interesting telephone call from a woman who works at the local animal shelter. She said that, some weeks ago, she received a call from our home phone number from someone named Seth, who asked about a certain dog that had been taken to the shelter by animal control."

Seth cringed, expecting a belated scolding, but his mother merely went on with her story. "When the woman at the animal shelter informed him that the dog had already been adopted out, this *person named Seth* expressed great disappointment. 'For him, it was that dog or none,' she told me. That's why she wrote down his name and phone number. 'Just in case,' she said."

Seth's mother laughed. "And what do you know, that *just in case* happened. Your furry friend ran away from his adopted home, only to get picked up a few days later by the animal control officer and taken back to the animal shelter. Because he had an ID tag, a shelter employee was able to contact his owner, who went to the shelter and retrieved him. But after the dog ran away for the fourth time, each time ending up back at the animal shelter, the owner decided he didn't want 'the mutt' anymore. 'He's too much trouble,' the owner insisted.

"Now here's the key part of the story," Seth's mother said, clearly enjoying telling it. "The woman at the shelter remembered the dog. But more importantly, she remembered your phone call and the anguish in your voice upon hearing that the dog had been adopted out. *Sooo*, she called here yesterday to let us know that the dog was again available for adoption.

"And *that*," his mother announced with a nod and a grin, "is how we got the dog."

"But Mom," Seth said, "I thought you didn't like him."

"Oh, sweetie," his mother replied, her voice ripe with caring, "that was before . . . well, you know."

"Before you knew he was my grandfather's dog."

She blushed. "Yes."

"Can I have a dog?" Baylie asked.

"Someday," their mother said, "when you're responsible enough to take care of one."

Baylie's frown made it clear that she wasn't happy with that answer, but at least she kept quiet about it.

"So what are you going to name your dog?" Seth's dad asked.

Seth stroked the dog's head. "He already has a name—Pond Dog."

"That's a stupid name," Baylie said.

"Bay-lie," Seth's mother said.

"Well, it is."

Seth ignored his sister. He cupped the dog's bearded muzzle in his hands and stared into those radiant canine eyes that seemed to say, *We belong together.* "I knew you wouldn't be happy anywhere else, Pond Dog."

The dog barked twice, reared up on its hind legs, and began licking Seth's face.

Seth's heart was filled with joy. "Mom," he said, "is it okay if I phone Collin and tell him to come over? I'm almost done with my homework."

"That's fine, sweetie."

"I'll tell him that I have a big surprise for him. He's always the one with the big surprises." He laughed. "He'll never guess."

Afterword

Since this book was written, but prior to its publication, interim Oregon State Representative Christine Goodwin, House District 2 (which includes part of Douglas County), announced her intention to sponsor a bill during the 2022 session of the Oregon State Legislature to ensure that unclaimed remains of a veteran or eligible descendant receive proper burial. According to a November 11, 2021 report of that announcement in *The News-Review* of Roseburg, Oregon:

> *That bill would direct the governing body of each county to designate a Veterans Service Officer to ensure interment of those remains. It would also require mortuaries and funeral homes to contact that officer when they have received remains.*
>
> *The veteran would then receive the honorable burial they had been promised by the U.S. Department of Veterans Affairs.*
>
> *"This is a long overdue recognition for veterans that no longer have family to claim their remains, give them burial, and honor their service to our country," Goodwin said.*

The author of this book lauds Representative Goodwin for her intention to sponsor such a bill, and sincerely hopes that when the bill is introduced it passes with unanimous support of our Oregon state legislators.

B. K. Mayo
Roseburg, Oregon   December 14, 2021

Acknowledgments

I want to thank Craig Kinney, Chief Medical-Legal Death Investigator for the Douglas County Medical Examiner's Office, for his invaluable assistance as I conducted my research for this book. He took the time to give me detailed descriptions of a drowning death investigation, from the time he arrives on the scene until the time the body is put into the medical examiner's truck. He even provided me with a picture of the truck—or "body wagon," as Collin called it. Any factual errors in the book relative to these procedures are mine.

I worked with two editors on this novel, Caroline Kaiser and Amaryah Orenstein, both of whom deserve credit for their discerning suggestions for improving the manuscript.

And once again, I am indebted to my wife, Karen, for committing herself to the task of reading and commenting on this novel from first draft to final rewrite, and for her unwavering support of me as a writer.

About the Author

On his quest to find the perfect job, B. K. Mayo worked as a fire alarm salesman, a steelworker, an IRS auditor, a park caretaker, a school bus driver, a library aide, a janitorial crew leader, an educational assistant, a special education teacher, and a high school detention room supervisor. He has now taken his rightful place in life as a full-time husband and novelist. He and his wife, Karen, live in an area of southwestern Oregon known as "the hundred valleys of the Umpqua."

For more about the author go to:
www.bkmayo.com